A Christmas PROMISE

K.C. WELLS

K.C. WELLS

Acknowledgments

A huge thank you, as always, to my wonderful team of betas:
Jason, Daniel, Helena, Mardee, Sharon, Debra and Will.

But special thanks go to Sharon D Simpson, for all her medical advice.

K.C. WELLS

Chapter One

New York, New York was belting out of the radio, and Micah Trant sang along, glad that his sister Naomi was nowhere nearby to hear him. Lord knew, she teased him enough about him knowing all the words to every Frank Sinatra song going. He laid the blame for that squarely at his Dad's door. Dad used to say it was evidence that he'd brought Micah up right.

Micah knew the truth. It was evidence, all right, but that Dad had played nothing *but* Sinatra when Micah was growing up. And driving alone along the silent roads, the banks of snow several feet above the road's gritty surface, Frank was a pretty good traveling companion, Micah had to admit. Wright was about twenty minutes away, and the road was deserted. It was almost eight o'clock and Micah should have been home hours ago. He smiled to himself. There was always the pull of 'one more photo', and once the sun had gone down, the snow had taken on an eerie glow that he'd been unable to resist. The idea of a nightscape appealed to him: so far, he hadn't done one of those.

Beside him on the passenger seat sat his most prized possession, his beloved Nikon, its memory card already half full of yet more images of Thunder Basin's snowy landscapes. He knew what his dad was going to say: 'What, more pictures of the snow? You've seen one, you've seen 'em all.' Then he'd flash that grin of his, just to let Micah know he was only teasing. Micah had overheard Dad bragging to Sherrie Longmire at the convenience store in Wright that his Micah was going to have an exhibition of paintings in Gillette the following year. It had tickled Micah to hear the pride in Dad's voice. Hard to believe it was the same man who'd blown a gasket all those years ago, when Micah had announced he wanted to be a painter. Still, he'd said nothing when Micah chose to study Art at college. Of course, by that time, Mom had worked her magic.

As always, the thought tightened his chest. The anniversary of her death was coming up real fast, and Micah looked forward to that time like he looked forward to root canal work. He and Naomi would be there for Dad, trying their damnedest to keep their own grief at bay. Christmas had lost its sparkle and charm the last few years, but that was hardly surprising: losing your mom on Christmas Day was a surefire way of making you yearn for New Year.

Micah sighed. At least he could get Thanksgiving out of the way before he started dreading Christmas.

Frank was singing about that toddlin' town, Chicago, when Micah spotted a dark shape ahead, by the side of the road. He instinctively slowed down to a crawl, hitting the brakes immediately when the car headlights picked out the splash of red against the snow.

What the hell? His skin went cold when he realized he was looking at a figure.

Micah reached into the glove box for his flashlight, and got out of the car, crunching over the grit and ice to where the figure lay huddled, half in the road. He focused the beam on the still form, whose face was hidden beneath the dark coat's hood. Micah crouched down beside the… body?… praying that there was still life present. Gently, he pulled the hood aside, revealing the bloodied face of a young man, maybe his own age. His eyes were swollen shut, blackened and bruised, and there were cuts and bruises to his cheeks and jaw. Micah did a quick appraisal of the rest of him. He couldn't tell if there were any broken bones, but thankfully, the guy was still breathing.

Micah stood up, trying to clear his thoughts. Memorial Hospital was probably the closest, but there was no way he could get hold of help: the phone signal was for shit on that road. So that meant no helicopter. His only other option was to lift the guy and put him in the car, on the back seat. Not that Micah liked that option at all. Lifting him could worsen what fractures and breaks he might already have, not to mention other possible injuries.

He stared at the prone figure, his gut roiling. "I'm guessing this is a risk I'm gonna have to take," he muttered to himself. He opened the back door as wide as he could, thankful for the two blankets he kept on the seat.

Now for the tricky part.

As carefully as he could, Micah eased the figure onto his back, before slipping one arm under his neck and the other under his knees. He gently lifted the young man, breathing heavily from the effort, and praying he wasn't doing more damage. Getting him onto the seat proved the hardest part, and he had to do that in two stages, reaching in from the other side to pull him across as gingerly as he could. Once he had the guy covered with both blankets, Micah closed both doors, making sure he wasn't about to crunch a limb in the process, and got back behind the wheel. What bothered him most was not once had the guy regained consciousness.

Micah drove as fast as his snow tires would allow, but it was still getting on for over an hour by the time he pulled up in front of the hospital, his heartbeat racing.

Please, still be alive, okay?

He yanked open the main door and ran into the warmth. "Help! I need help out here! It's urgent!" A couple of orderlies responded instantly, and he pointed out to the car. "Unconscious, in the snow, been like this for over an hour, possible broken bones."

He watched as his passenger was wheeled into the hospital on a gurney, heading for the ER. Micah went out to park the car in the first space he could find. He placed his bag in the trunk, then ran back into the hospital, following the direction the orderlies had taken. When he reached the desk in the ER, a nurse told him the guy had been taken straight in for assessment.

"Do you know him?"

Micah shook his head. "I found him by the road, about twenty minutes from Wright. I figured this was the best place for him." The clinic in Wright was okay, but they weren't equipped to deal with something like this.

"Okay, please take a seat. The police will want to talk to you. I'm just going to call them."

"Police?"

She nodded, her eyes kind. "We don't know what happened to him, but he's clearly been beaten up. He's in no state to tell us anything, and since you can't give us any information, we have to notify the police."

That made sense. "Okay." Then it occurred to him that his dad would be going crazy right then. "I just need to make a call."

"Sure." Her face fell. "Poor guy. Someone sure made a mess of him."

Micah had been thinking the same thing. *How could someone leave him like that?*

"Maybe whoever robbed him thought he was dead," she suggested.

"If it *was* robbery." There were other options that Micah didn't want to think about.

He reached into his pocket for his phone and sighed when he saw the screen. Several missed calls, all from Dad.

Shit. He'd forgotten he'd had the phone on silent. He speed-dialed home.

"Where are you?" His dad sounded gruff. "We expected you home hours ago. I tried calling you a while back, but got nothing."

"Yeah, the signal was lousy, and then I put it on silent. Dad, listen." Micah took a deep breath. "I found a guy by the roadside, all beaten up. I brought him to Memorial Hospital."

"Aww, Christ. Is he all right?" Micah caught the concern in his voice.

"He's in the ER right now. I have to stay, because the police will want to talk to me. If it gets too late, I'll see if I can find a bed or a chair for the night. I'll let you know, all right?"

"Sure thing. Poor guy. Glad you found him. God, I hope he makes it."

Micah hoped so too.

Two police officers had come and gone, after questioning Micah thoroughly about the state the guy had been in, where exactly Micah had found him, and what had made him stop in the first place. They told him detectives would return the following day to check on the guy, to question him if he regained consciousness.

Micah sat on a chair, darting glances toward the door where he knew the young man was being treated. *What are they doing in there? How long does it take to make sure he's gonna be okay?*

"Hey, honey?" He looked up, to find a girl holding out a plastic cup of something steaming. "Here. It's just a little hot chocolate. You look like you need it."

Micah smiled. "Thanks. That's really kind of you."

She returned his smile, her cheeks dimpling. "You're welcome." Then she walked toward the desk, waving at the nurse behind it. Micah's perusal was interrupted when a doctor came through the doors he'd been staring at, heading for Micah.

"Mr. Trant?"

Micah put down his cup on the chair beside him, and got to his feet. "How is he?"

"Unfortunately, I can't give out that information."

"Can't you at least tell me if he's going to be okay?" Micah had sort of anticipated that response, but it still frustrated him.

The doctor's expression was grave. "To be honest, he's a very lucky young man. It could have been much worse."

"Can... can I see him?"

The doctor smiled. "Once he's settled in ICU, a nurse will take you to him. He's very fortunate that you found him when you did." He patted Micah on the arm and went back through the doors.

Micah retook his seat and sipped his hot beverage. He didn't care what time it was: all he wanted was to see the guy breathing, to hear the reassuring beep of a heart monitor.

He could wait all night for that.

The only sounds in ICU were the beeping and whirring of the machines that were doing their all-important jobs of keeping patients alive. The nurse showed him to the bed in the corner, where Micah recognized the guy instantly. Tubes trailed over the bed, which was lit by a light on the wall above it. The stark light did nothing to lessen the impact: the guy looked awful. His injured left leg was supported by what seemed to be a pulley system of weights and counterweights, and his head was bandaged.

"How is he?" Micah whispered.

"He'd been drifting in and out of consciousness since they brought him here."

"Ugh." The pain-ridden sound came from the bed.

Micah stepped closer. "Hey," he said softly. "You're in a hospital. You're badly hurt."

The guy attempted to open one eye, but winced from the effort. The nurse went around to the other side of his bed, checking his pulse and blood pressure. "You don't have to talk now, okay?" she said softly.

"Ugh." Another sound laced with pain.

Micah want to place a hand on the guy to reassure him, but he had no idea if that would hurt him. "Easy. You've got a lot of bruising, and your leg is in a bad way, but you're gonna be okay." At least, Micah fervently hoped so.

"Robbed?" he croaked.

The nurse bent over him. "We don't know for sure. The docs didn't find much on you. No ID, but I'm guessing that was in your wallet, and they didn't find that either. Right now, you're a John Doe."

In spite of the obvious pain, the guy struggled to open his eyes. "Greg. Greg Chambers." His breathing hitched. "Backpack? Envelope?"

"You didn't have a backpack when I found you. Envelope? What envelope?" Micah bent lower. "Is it important?"

Greg attempted to nod, wincing again.

"Easy now," the nurse soothed. "You need to rest. We've given you something for the pain, and it should help you sleep."

"No… you don't understand… have to find him… made a promise." A low moan escaped Greg's lips, probably from the effort of speaking those few words.

The nurse reacted instantly. "Okay, sir? You need to calm down."

"His name is Greg," Micah told her. Greg's obvious distress tore at him.

She nodded. "Okay, Greg? You need to let the painkillers do their job. Try to sleep, all right? We'll take care of you." She laid a hand on his forehead, her eyes kind.

Micah watched as the drugs finally got to work, and Greg slipped into a deep sleep. His words were still on Micah's mind, however.

"Where did his stuff go? His clothes?"

The nurse frowned. "They had to cut off his clothing in the ER. Whatever else he had is probably at the nurse's station down the hall." She peered at Micah. "He'll be asleep for hours. You can go if you like."

Micah was torn. On the one hand he knew Dad would already be stressing about him, but on the other, he didn't want to leave Greg. "Can I stay a while longer? Just a little while?" He gave her his most winning smile.

The nurse hesitated, but Micah could tell he'd won her over. "Okay, seeing as you're the one who probably saved his life. I'll be back to check on him in fifteen minutes."

Micah thanked her, then waited until she'd left the room. He gazed down at Greg, who appeared to be sound asleep. *What envelope?* Whatever it was, it had clearly distressed him. Micah's curiosity got the better of him, and he walked quietly to the door, stepping out into the hallway.

At the end of the hall was a wide desk, and Micah headed for it. The nurse on duty glanced up as he approached. "Can I help you?"

"I'm here with the guy who was just brought up from the ER. He seems to be worrying about something. Do you have his personal effects?"

She regarded him suspiciously. "Yes, but why do you want to see them?"

"He came to just now, and was asking if he'd been robbed. He mentioned an envelope. Seemed kinda important to him." Micah held up his hands. "Hey, *you* can be the one to go through his belongings, if it makes you feel more comfortable. I just want to see if whoever beat him up, took this envelope too. They took his wallet."

She bit her lip. "I suppose it's okay, as long as you stay here." She pulled open a deep drawer, took out the dark hooded jacket Micah recalled, and placed it on the desk. "Take a look."

Micah slipped his hands into the outer pockets, but they were empty, so he peered inside. There was a zipped pocket. Micah opened it and felt inside, his fingers touching paper. He removed a folded envelope. "Looks like they didn't get this." Then he unfolded the envelope, and—

What the fuck?

Micah stared at the scrawled writing, trying to get his head around it.

"What's wrong?" the nurse asked. "You look like you've seen a ghost."

Micah swallowed. "I don't understand this." He held out the envelope, so she could read what was written on it.

She squinted and read aloud, "Joshua Trant, Wright, Campbell County, Wyoming." She raised her eyebrows. "What's strange about that?

Micah fished out his ID and held it up for her to see. "Look, my name's Micah Trant. Joshua Trant… is my dad."

Her eyes widened. "Oh wow. And you found him? What are the odds on that?"

Micah wasn't thinking about the odds. He was thinking about making an urgent call.

"Look, can I keep hold of this?"

She bit her lip. "I'm sorry. Regardless of whether it's addressed to your father or not, it *is* the property of the patient. When he's awake, he can decide what to do with it." She held out her hand for the envelope.

Reluctantly, Micah handed it over. "I'll be back in a short while. I just have to make a call." He left her and walked briskly down the hallway, heading for the main door. Outside in the frigid air, he shivered as he speed-dialed.

"How is he?" Dad asked as soon as the call connected.

"He's got a lot of injuries. Right now, he's sedated. But that's not why I'm calling. Before he passed out, he said something about an envelope, finding someone, and a promise. Well, I found the envelope." Micah still didn't believe it.

"Yeah?"

"It only has a name written on it, and a town." Micah drew in another deep breath. "Dad, it's… your name."

Silence followed. Finally, his dad spoke. "Seriously?"

"Uh huh. Joshua Trant, Wright, Campbell County, Wyoming."

"This guy got a name?"

"Yeah, Greg Chambers."

"Nah, doesn't ring a bell." Another pause. "You're not kidding, are you? This isn't a joke, is it?"

"Would I kid you about something like this?"

Dad huffed. "I'm grabbing my keys. I'm on my way."

Micah blinked. "Dad? It's real late. You should be going to bed soon. Besides, what can you do here? He's asleep."

"Then I'll nap in a chair until he wakes up. You think I can sleep after this? The guy's got an envelope addressed to me. Of *course* I wanna know what this is all about. I'll be there as fast as I can."

"Hey, drive carefully, okay? The roads are

getting icy again." Micah's stomach clenched at the thought of his dad veering off the road and into a snowbank. Or worse.

"Don't you fret, I'll be careful. See you soon." Dad disconnected.

Micah pocketed his phone and went back into the building. He hurried to ICU and tapped on the glass door to attract the nurse's attention.

She opened it. "I thought you'd gone."

"Am I okay to come back in?"

She smiled. "Sure, but he's still asleep."

Micah walked over to Greg's bed and stared down at him. *Who are you?* There was clearly a mystery here.

The nurse stood beside him. "His vital signs are slightly better. They should be able to fix his leg tomorrow." She glanced at Micah. "You don't need to stay."

Micah took a deep breath. "Thing is, my dad's on his way here, and it'll take him at least an hour and a half. So… can I stay? I'll sit in that chair over in the corner. I promise I won't be in your way." Micah did the best impression of Bambi that he could manage, all wide-eyed and innocent.

The nurse bit back a smile. "You're cute when you do that." She sighed. "Okay, fine. But if the doctor comes back and wants you out of here, that's it, all right?"

He nodded enthusiastically. "Thank you…" He scanned her name badge and smiled. "Rachel. Thank you, Rachel."

The way Rachel was looking at him gave Micah a sinking feeling he might have overdone the charm. Too bad that sweet expression wouldn't get her very far. Rachel was definitely not his type, the major black mark against her being the fact that her plumbing was all wrong, as far as he was concerned.

Rachel beamed. "You're welcome. You might not be thanking me when you sit for a while in that chair, however." She left the room, her hips swaying a little more than previously.

Micah shook his head. *Nice girl. Too bad it won't get her anywhere with me.* He sat down in the chair, and closed his eyes.

Chapter Two

"Micah. *Micah!*"

Micah awoke with a start. "Wha?"

Dad stared down at him, his hand on Micah's shoulder. "Hey, sleepyhead."

Micah sat up straight, rubbing his eyes. "What time is it?"

"A little after one. The nurse let me in here." He held up an insulated cup. "Want some coffee?"

Micah groaned. "You're a lifesaver. The stuff from those machines is just nasty." He flipped open the closure on the lid and inhaled the steaming liquid, before glancing around. "Where is the nurse, by the way?"

"She just stepped out for a moment." Dad wandered over to the bed, gazing down at Greg. "Never seen this kid before in my life."

Micah took a sip of hot coffee and let out a contented sigh. "Yeah, that's what I'm talking about." He got up out of the chair and joined him. "Kid? He's probably about the same age as me."

Dad grinned. "I rest my case." He went back to studying Greg. "God, he's skinny. There's nothing to him."

"You sure you don't know anyone by the name of Chambers?"

Dad shook his head. "I'm trying to see if he looks like anyone I know, but it's so hard to tell with all that bruising." He expelled a long breath. "Still can't quite believe this, you finding him, and him with an envelope with my name on it. Where is that, by the way?"

"The nurse outside has it. She said it's up to Greg to give it to you, if that's what he wants."

Dad sighed. "Then we're gonna wait until he's awake. I mean, I know it has to be for me—there's only one Joshua Trant in Wright, at least as far as I know."

Micah chuckled at that. There had to be less than two thousand souls in Wright. Not the smallest town in Wyoming, not even in the top five, and certainly bigger than Buford on I-80, that boasted it was the 'Smallest Town in America', with nothing but a single house and a gas station.

Dad shook his head. "Poor kid. Wonder who did this to him, and why?"

"He was robbed." Micah regarded Greg for a

moment, taking in the movement beneath his eyelids and the occasional soft whimpers that fell from his lips.

"Nope, not buying it," Dad stated emphatically. "Why not just throw a punch and knock him out, then rob him?" He pointed to Greg's leg, held in traction. "No, son, there's malice here." He yawned, covering his mouth with his hand.

"Here, sit in the chair and try to sleep." Micah guided him to the corner. "I'll clear it with Rachel." When his dad arched his eyebrows, heat spread up Micah's neck and face. "The nurse, I mean."

Dad chuckled. "You had me worried for a moment there. I thought you'd gone over to the other side of the church."

"Hush. Get some sleep." Micah waited until his dad was in the chair before looking around for another. When he didn't find a spare one, he left the room. Rachel was at the desk, staring at a monitor. She glanced up as Micah approached, and smiled.

"Aw, did your dad wake you up? You were sleeping so soundly."

Micah nodded. "If it's okay, we're going to stay until Greg wakes up. Can I find another chair somewhere?" He waited, holding his breath that he hadn't pushed her good nature too far.

Rachel hesitated, then nodded. "Sure. Grab a chair from the waiting room. Just be sure not to disturb him, okay? He needs his rest."

"Of course, and thanks." Micah went on a chair hunt, and pretty soon he was carrying one back to ICU. Dad was already asleep when he got there, his head supported on his hand as he leaned on the chair arm. Micah smiled to himself as he set down his chair next to

Dad's. He sat in it and gazed across to where Greg was sleeping.

This is crazy. We're waiting for a stranger to wake up and tell us what was so important about finding Dad. Micah had hoped Dad would have seem something familiar about Greg, but the state he was in, Micah doubted Greg's own mother would have recognized him.

A warm fuzziness stole over him, and Micah fell asleep.

"No… get off me…. Stop…."

Micah blinked, not sure if he was still dreaming.

"I won't… please… stop."

The pain in Greg's voice was enough to jolt any tiredness from him, and he lunged up from his chair and over to the bed. Greg was frowning, his hands clenching and unclenching on top of the blanket, sweat popping out on his brow, his breathing labored.

Micah didn't hesitate. He reached for the button to summon help.

A minute later, Rachel was at Greg's side, checking the IV drip and looking at his chart. She quickly took his temperature and gently lifted his eyelids to examine his pupils. Then she disappeared briefly, only to return with a small vial. Micah watched as she injected some of its contents into the IV tube. The result was almost instantaneous: Greg's breathing evened out and his fists unclenched.

Rachel gazed at him, stroking his forehead as she checked his pulse.

"Was he… dreaming?" Micah got the feeling it had been a nightmare. "He was talking in his sleep. Sounded like he was fighting someone off."

She sighed. "The pain meds were wearing off. He'll sleep more soundly now." She glanced at her watch. "It's almost five am. I'll be going off duty soon. I'll make sure the nurse who takes over knows you're here." Another glance at Greg. "He seems calmer now." She smiled at Micah. "Any chance I can get your number before I go?" Her cheeks were flushed. "It's not like you're even related to the patient, so I wouldn't get in trouble for asking." Her eyes sparkled. "Maybe we could go out for a coffee or something."

Aw crap. Micah struggled for the words to let her down gently.

"Sorry, honey, but he's spoken for. There's a girl at home, waiting for him." Dad sounded groggy, but his tone was apologetic.

"Oh, okay." Rachel bit her lip. "I thought I'd ask, seeing as you weren't wearing a ring. Never mind. These days, if you don't ask, you don't get, my mom says." She gave Micah a pat on the arm and left the room.

Micah waited until he was sure she was out of earshot, before turning slowly to stare at his dad. "There's a girl at home?" He was trying hard not to laugh.

Dad shrugged. "That wasn't a lie. There *is* a girl at home right now, but cute nurse here doesn't need to know it's your sister. Besides, what if you told her you were gay, and she turned out to be one of those haters you hear so much about?"

Micah had to admire his dad's thought processes.

He gazed down at Greg. "I wonder who he was fighting off?"

Dad joined him. "Let's face it, he's not gonna have just medical issues to deal with. We could be talking PTSD here. Boy could have nightmares about this for the rest of his life."

"Aw, don't say that." The idea made Micah's heart ache for Greg.

His dad tugged on his elbow. "How about you go find us some coffee, while I stay with Greg?" He grinned. "You drank all the stuff I brought."

Micah arched his eyebrows. "I think you should try to get a little more sleep while you can."

Dad shook his head. "I'm fine. Besides, all I can think about is what's in that damned envelope."

Micah couldn't blame him for that. He was more than a little curious himself. "Then I'll go fetch coffee. But you have been warned."

"That bad, huh?" Dad let out a chuckle. "I'll cope."

Micah laughed quietly and went off in search of hot liquid trying to pass itself off as coffee.

"Micah!"

He woke with a start. "Huh? Did I fall asleep?" He had no idea of the time.

Dad stared down at him. "Son, Greg is awake."

Micah blinked. "Really? Oh. Okay." He rubbed

his eyes and then got to his feet. A new nurse was standing beside Greg's bed, doing her observations. She smiled as they approached.

"The doctor will be here shortly, so don't wear him out, all right?" She gave Greg a last glance before walking away from the bed.

Micah gazed at Greg. "Hey. Remember me from last night?"

Greg gave a single nod. "You're the guy that brought me here. Thank you so much." He spoke carefully, his mouth swollen.

"Anyone would've done the same," Micah said with a shrug. "I hope you don't mind, but the nurse let me go through your jacket. You mentioned an envelope?"

Greg stilled. "Is it… still there?"

He nodded. "Yeah, only…" Micah took a deep breath. "The name on the envelope? Joshua Trant?"

"Yes?"

Dad stepped closer. "Greg, I'm Micah's father. I'm Joshua Trant."

Greg's eyes widened, and his mouth fell open. "Seriously?"

Dad nodded. "So, you can probably guess how curious I am right now. We've never met, have we?"

"No, sir." Greg swallowed. "But… I made a promise to find you. I—"

"I'm sorry." The nurse appeared at his bedside. "You'll have to step outside while the doctor examines Greg."

"Can… can they stay?" Greg asked suddenly. "If I say it's okay by me?"

"Not really," she said firmly.

"Then… what if I give the doctor permission

to… discuss my case with them, once he's seen me? Would that be all right?"

Micah stared at him, surprised by the request.

The nurse sighed. "Very well. But they still have to leave."

Micah grabbed his dad by the arm. "Come on, let's go." He gave Greg a smile. "We'll be right back, okay?"

Greg nodded. "Good."

Micah led his dad out of ICU. Outside, he leaned against the wall, yawning. "What time is it anyway?"

"Eight." Dad shivered. "I was talking to the nurse while you were asleep. She was telling me what they generally do in cases like this. He'll probably have to have pins and a plate put in his leg to repair the fracture." Dad scowled. "Makes me wonder, how he got such an injury in the first place. Because she said it looked to her like his thigh got stomped on." He shook his head. "Kid's damn lucky the bone didn't break in two."

"That sounds nasty." Micah peered through the glass to where the doctor and the nurse were standing by Greg's bed, their expressions neutral. He couldn't see Greg, however. "Still, he looks better than he did last night." At least he was talking coherently.

"You know what worries me? How's he gonna pay for all this? He's just a kid. And he doesn't look like he's loaded."

Micah had reached the same conclusion. Movement caught his eye. "Hey. Doc's coming."

A moment later, the doctor had left the ICU and was standing in front of them. "He's stable enough for surgery, and the orthopedist has booked the OR, so we're ready to take him down. It's a simple enough fracture to repair. We'll dress the wound, then we'll fit him with a knee immobilizer before he's discharged, that he'll wear while the leg heals."

"How long will he be in here?" Dad asked.

"Seven to ten days. He'll need physical therapy though, once he's been discharged." The doctor smiled. "I'll be around later to see how he's doing." He left them and walked off down the hallway. A minute or two later, two orderlies appeared and entered the ICU.

"Wow, they don't mess around, do they?" Dad muttered as Greg was wheeled out of ICU. He managed a single wave of his hand before disappearing out of sight around the corner.

The nurse came out to speak with them. "They've taken him down to the OR. You might want to visit the cafeteria and grab a bite to eat while he's having surgery. You've been here all night, so you must be hungry. But don't hurry back. He's going to be in there two hours minimum, and it could be as long as six, once he's out of recovery."

Dad's face fell. "That long?"

"It's difficult to predict. But hey, there's a visitor's lounge on the first floor." She winked. "The chairs are a lot more comfortable than the ones in ICU. If you want to stay, why don't you go there?" With a friendly smile, she went back into ICU.

Dad's belly rumbled, and Micah chuckled. "Good advice. Let's see what they have in the way of breakfast. A couple of pancakes and some coffee sounds good right now."

As they walked along the hallway, Dad gave a backward glance toward ICU. "I sure wanna know what's in that envelope."

"I know, and I'm positive you'll find out, once Greg's had his surgery. He'd have probably given it to you just then, if the doc hadn't showed up."

Dad shook his head. "Wanna know something funny? Now he's awake? There's something a little… familiar about him, like I've seen him before." He gave a shrug. "Well, I'll know soon enough." He rubbed his hands together briskly. "I'm starving."

Micah rolled his eyes. "When are you not? No wonder Naomi thinks you have a tapeworm."

Dad grimaced. "Hey, don't go saying stuff like that when we're in a hospital. That's just plain wrong."

He chuckled. "I hope the cafeteria has enough food to satisfy that humongous appetite of yours." His mind was focused on Greg, however. Micah couldn't help wondering what the hell was going on.

Micah yawned as they walked along the hallway to ICU.

Dad snickered. "Haven't you had enough sleep?" He counted off on his fingers. "You were asleep when I got here, then you dozed off again…and for God's sake, you just slept for three hours. I swear, someone snatched my son and exchanged him for Rip Van Winkle." Thankfully whatever else he was going to say got cut short when Dad's phone burst into life. "Oh hell. It's your sister."

Micah snickered. "I'm glad she's calling you and

not me." Naomi was a worrier, a trait she'd inherited from Mom. Not that he minded all that much: it was like Mom hadn't truly gone.

Except of course, she had.

Micah pushed the thought from his mind, and glanced across at his dad. It suddenly occurred to him why Naomi was calling. She had to be going out of her mind, since neither of them had called home.

"Naomi, I'm fine." Dad caught Micah's glance and rolled his eyes. "Yes, I agree, I should have left you a note, but I was in a hurry, and I forgot." He sighed. "Yes, I know one of us should have called, but… we fell asleep."

Micah heard her snort from three feet away.

"Look, I'm fine, Micah's fine. Remember I told you he found a guy by the roadside last night, all beat up? Well, we've just got a call to say he's out of surgery, and we're waiting to see how he's doing… Yes, we'll both be home later. How about you get some of that soup you made last weekend out of the freezer? We'll have that when we get home… Yeah, sure, I'll tell him. Later, sweetheart." He disconnected and huffed out a breath.

"Sounds like she was giving you the third degree," Micah remarked with amusement.

Dad lifted his eyebrows. "Oh, you may well smirk, mister. *You* are in big trouble."

"Me? What did I do?"

"Apparently, *you* were supposed to stop me from dashing out into the snow, risking life and limb to drive to the hospital. *You* were supposed to make me stay at home. And to top it all, *you* didn't call her." Dad's eyes twinkled.

Micah snorted. "Hey, you have a phone too. And

as for the rest… Yeah, right. Since when can either of us stop you from doing *anything*, once your mind is made up?" He glanced up to see the nurse standing outside the door of ICU.

"Greg is out of surgery." She smiled. "He's still groggy, but he wants to see you. So if you'll come with me? We've moved him to another bed now."

They followed her along the hallway to the elevator. "He's on the second floor. The nurse at the desk knows to expect you." The doors slid open and she gave them a warm smile. "Thank you again for all you did for him," she said to Micah. The doors shut, and the elevator whirred smoothly into action.

When they got out at the correct floor, the nurse's station was facing them. A nurse directed them to the room at the end of the hallway, which contained two beds, one of which was empty.

Greg was sitting in bed, leaning back against the pillows, his eyes closed. In his hand was the creased envelope. As they approached the bed, he blinked several times. "Hey. Lookit me. 'M all truss' up like a turkey." He indicated his leg, which was encased in bandages.

It was obvious from his slurred speech that he wasn't fully awake.

"Do you want us to come back later when you've had some rest?" Micah asked.

Greg shook his head. "Nah. Want to talk to you."

The nurse appeared at the foot of his bed. "The doctor says he could be out of here in just over a week." She smiled at Micah. "And he sounds sleepy because the drugs are working."

"And where will you go then?" Dad asked. "Where is home?"

Greg closed his eyes again. "Good question. Not sure I know anymore." Before Micah could decipher the cryptic remark, Greg opened one eye and held out the envelope. "For you, sir."

Dad took it. "Feels like we need a drum roll or something," he joked, but Micah could see from the tension in his jaw that he was nervous. He tore it open and pulled out a couple of sheets of folded paper, covered in handwriting. After a moment, Dad's jaw dropped, and he looked up sharply at Greg. "Your dad?"

Greg nodded, his gaze locked on Dad's face. "Made me promise to find you, to make sure you got it. This was… very important."

Dad sank into the nearby chair, the letter clutched in hands that trembled slightly.

"Do you know what it says?" Micah asked Greg quietly, disconcerted by his dad's state.

Greg shook his head, looking more awake. "All he told me was to deliver it in person. He—" His eyes widened, and a look of anguish contorted his face. "Oh God."

Micah followed his gaze, and his heart almost stopped at the sight.

His dad was crying.

Chapter Three

"Dad?" Micah was frozen to the spot. He'd only ever seen his father cry once, and that had been the day Mom died. At the funeral, it had been as though he'd kept a tight grip on his emotions. Micah had expected tears, anger, frustration, but instead had been met with a calm that was almost frightening. Watching the tears crawl down his dad's cheeks now was torture.

Dad glanced up, savagely wiping away the moisture with his hand. "Stupid old fool. Blubbering like some snot-nosed kid. Ignore me." He regarded the letter, holding it limply in his hands.

Whatever Micah had wanted to say was lost when a young man came into the room, carrying a clipboard. "Mr. Chambers? We need your address and insurance information."

Greg's face fell. "Oh. Yeah, of course."

Micah caught the flash of panic across Greg's face.

Dad jerked his head up. "Are we talking hospital bills? I'll take care of those." He straightened in his chair.

Micah stared at him. *What the hell?*

"Excuse me, but no." Greg spoke quietly, but there was a hard edge to his voice, as if he was trying his utmost to shake off the effects of the drugs. "You don't know me from Adam, and there's no way I'm going to let a complete stranger take on my debts." He set his jaw and met Dad's gaze with a resolute stare. He swallowed. "I'll need to make a phone call first."

Dad lurched to his feet. "No, Greg. I'll foot the bill. It's the least I can do for... Hayden's son."

The billing clerk gave a discreet cough. "If this is a bad time, I can come back later."

Dad gave him a smile. "That might be best." The clerk nodded and left the room.

Micah blinked as several thoughts collided in his head. *Hayden? Did he save Dad's life? Donate a kidney? Introduce him to Mom? Who the hell is Hayden?*

Dad took another glance at the letter before meeting Greg's gaze. "He *is* dead then."

"Yes, sir." Greg swallowed hard. "Last month."

"I see. Well, that doesn't change anything. I still want to do this." When Greg made an unhappy sound,

Dad turned to him. "Please. You have to let me do this."

Heaven knew what Greg saw in his dad's face, because Greg stilled, as immobile as a statue. "Okay," he whispered. "But… promise me we'll talk about this?"

Dad nodded. "I promise. And when they discharge you? You're coming home with us."

Greg's mouth fell open. "I can't… I mean, I—" He snapped his mouth shut.

Dad gave a slow nod. "When you can't even say where your home is? Yeah, right. Like I'm gonna let you just leave. Not Hayden's child. No, sir. You're gonna need to recuperate, probably for a couple of weeks at least, and you can do that in our home. We'll make sure you're looked after."

Micah saw the range of emotions that crossed Greg's face, and sighed. "Don't even try to argue with him. You'll lose, every time. And I speak from experience."

Greg gave a half smile. "I believe you. Besides, I recognize that expression. I saw it enough times on my dad's face when he…" He took a breath. "Never mind."

Dad got to his feet. "We're gonna go home now, but we'll be back later, all right? Once we know what the visiting hours are. Is there anything you'd like us to bring you?"

Greg shrugged. "Something to read? They… stole my backpack, so I've got nothing, not even clothes."

Dad nodded. "Leave that to me. What do you like to read?"

"Murder mysteries." Greg smiled. "I was kind of brought up on Agatha Christie."

Micah laughed. "Oh, I think we might be able to find you something, right, Dad?"

Dad gave him a sharp look. "Very funny." He turned to Greg. "I have a couple of Agatha Christies at home." Micah snorted, and Dad speared him with a glare. "Okay, more than a couple."

Even Greg managed a chuckle. "That would be great, thank you."

Micah held out his hand. "Later, yeah?"

Greg clasped it firmly. "Sure. Thanks again." He released Micah's hand and sank back into the pillows.

"Mr. Chambers? There are two detectives here to speak to you." The nurse stood in the doorway.

"And that's our cue," Dad said, patting Greg on the shoulder. "See you later, okay?" He straightened and headed for the door, Micah following, just as two guys entered the room, one of them clutching a black backpack, the shoulder strap torn away at one point.

"Oh my God, you found it!" The joy in Greg's voice was impossible to miss. "Thank you."

Micah paused at the threshold, watching as Greg opened the pack, delved inside it, and brought out a wooden carved box, wrapped in cellophane. Greg stared at it, his chest rising and falling rapidly, making no move to open it.

That box was clearly important.

"Come on." Dad tugged his elbow. "You want Naomi more pissed at us than she already is?"

Micah chuckled. "Good point. Let's go home."

"But first, we're gonna stop by Billing, once we know where it is."

That didn't come as a surprise to Micah. Dad could be stubborn when he wanted to be. The mystery of Greg's box would have to wait until they returned. Right then, he had another riddle waiting to be solved.

A CHRISTMAS PROMISE

Who was Hayden, and why was he so important to my Dad, that he'd pay for Greg's hospital bills?

Micah knew why he couldn't sleep, of course. Dad hadn't said a word so far about the letter. Not a single goddamn word. They'd driven home separately, but once they were inside the house, Micah had fully expected his dad to sit down and tell him everything.

Nope. Not even close. Dad had simply gotten on with his day, withdrawing into his office to work on his software designs. Even that was weird. Naomi was home for the weekend, and usually that meant Dad didn't work, but spent time with her. Micah could tell by the perplexed glances she kept throwing at the closed office door, that Naomi was at a loss too. Dad emerged for lunch and dinner, but that was all they saw of him for the rest of the day.

No wonder I'm not sleeping. Too much going on around here that's upsetting the routine.

Lying in bed staring at the ceiling was accomplishing nothing, so Micah decided to get up and make himself a warm drink. Maybe that would help. He threw back the covers and hastily pulled on his robe, before the chill night air got to his… extremities. He put on a pair of thick socks and crept out of his room, heading for the stairs down to the kitchen and praying he'd miss the one stair that always creaked. But when he reached the bottom, he saw the light seeping from under the door to Dad's office.

Huh?

Micah walked as silently as he could up to the door, and opened it. The room was bathed in the warm light of the corner lamp, and Dad was sitting on the small couch beside it, his robe tied around the waist. In his lap was the letter and what looked like a strip of photos, like the ones you got in photo booths.

Dad jerked his head up, and Micah saw the tracks of tears on his cheeks.

"Why aren't you asleep?" Dad wiped his face hastily. "Do you know what time it is?"

"I couldn't sleep," Micah explained. "I was actually worrying about you. And now that I see you?" His heartbeat raced. "Yep, still worried." He came fully into the room. "Dad, what's going on?"

"Nothing." Dad folded the letter, slipping the photo strip inside it. "Go back to bed."

Micah had had enough. "Do *not* treat me like a child. Not when it's obvious that something is really wrong." He cocked his head. "Is it so bad that you can't tell me?"

Dad shivered. "What if… what if I tell you, and you find you can't look at me the same, ever again?"

"Is that what you're afraid of?" Micah gazed at him incredulously. "Well, unless you're about to confess to being a serial killer, I think it's a safe bet I'm gonna look at you the same as I've always done. You're my dad and I love you." He forced himself to take a couple of deep breaths. "So why don't I sit down, so you can tell me who this Hayden is—or was—why you just offered to pay a stranger's hospital bills, and why you're crying over that letter?"

Dad gulped. "I think… I'm gonna need a drink." He left the letter on the arm of the couch, got up, and walked over to his filing cabinet, on top of which sat a half full bottle of what looked like whiskey, and a glass. He gave Micah an apologetic glance. "I've only got the one glass, so if you want one, you'll have to fetch your own."

Micah waved his hand. "I'm fine, but you go ahead." If his dad needed fortifying, this had to be some revelation that was coming. He walked over to the couch and sat at the opposite end, pulling his legs up onto it, and grabbing a cushion to hug. Dad poured himself a glass, maybe a couple of fingers, and after screwing the cap back on, rejoined Micah on the couch.

He took a sip. "Do you know how long I've lived in Wyoming? Since I was seventeen. My parents moved here when your grandad got a new job in Casper. Before that? We lived in Sylacauga."

Micah frowned. "Where on earth is that?"

"In Alabama, on the edge of the Talladega Forest." He gave a wistful smile. "Great place to be a kid."

Despite the nervous knot in his belly, Micah smiled. "I know you said your family came from the South, but Alabama? You're a *real* Southern boy, aren't ya? Well, I guess that explains Granddad's and Grandma's accent. It's a whole lot stronger than yours."

Dad chuckled. "I think I lost mine years ago."

"I catch a twang every now and then." Micah wondered where this was leading. "Okay, you've started now, so keep talking."

Dad regarded him in silence for a moment, then removed the strip of photos and handed it to Micah. He gazed at the images of two young men. They were clearly goofing off in a couple, laughing and pulling funny faces. But that last two photos… Micah peered more closely. "That's you, isn't it? The guy in the blue shirt?"

Dad nodded. "I was seventeen. That was taken maybe three or four months before we left Alabama."

Micah stared at his dad's image, caught by… something. Maybe it was the way his dad was looking at the other guy, the almost tangible connection between them. Then it clicked.

"This is Hayden, isn't it?" When Dad didn't respond, Micah looked up. "Dad?"

He sighed. "Yeah, that was Hayden. We were the same age. We'd known each other all our lives, ever since kindergarten."

That might have accounted for the closeness between the two, but… Micah looked again, only this time he put aside the thought that this was his dad, and tried to view it objectively. That was when the significance of the looks they were giving each other hit him like a blow to the stomach. It was so obvious.

"You were in love with him."

Dad flinched. "How do you know?"

Micah sighed. "Dad, I may be gay, but that doesn't mean I'm dumb. Or deaf, or blind, for that matter. The way he's staring at you…."

"How? How is he staring at me?" The pain in his dad's voice was almost too much to bear.

"Like you hung the moon," Micah said simply. He placed the strip of photos on the seat cushion next to his dad.

Dad sagged against the cushions. "I've looked at these photos so many times over the years. I tried to tell myself that none of it was real, that it was a phase, that I didn't really love him, heart, body and soul. But then I'd look at his face, that expression, and I'd know I was lying to myself."

Micah shifted closer. "Dad, what happened?" he asked softly. His mind was still reeling from the fact that his dad had loved a guy. Micah's world had just tilted a little on its axis.

Dad took a long drink from his glass. "I was over at Hayden's house one evening. We were studying for a test. His parents had gone out to see some friends, and we didn't expect them back for hours." He forced out a bitter laugh. "Turned out they'd gotten halfway there, and his mom remembered something she'd forgotten. I can't even recall what it was now. All I know is, they came back early."

"Oh God. They didn't catch you guys in bed or something?"

Dad swallowed. "No. We never got that far. They found us on his bed though, fully clothed, but… kissing." He met Micah's gaze, his eyes misted over. "Do you know how many times I've regretted that they turned up when they did? We'd finally decided to… that is, he'd have been… my first."

For one second, they were no longer father and son, but two men, sharing an intimate moment that both could understand.

"Seventeen. Wow." Micah shook his head. "Compared to you, I'm definitely a late bloomer."

"And before you even *think* about pointing out that we were underage, all I'm gonna say is, if you're telling me kids that age aren't having sex nowadays, I—"

"No, no, I wasn't going to say a thing!" Micah protested. "Please. Keep going. What happened next?" Judging from his dad's emotional state, it had to be something pretty drastic.

"Hayden's dad grabbed hold of me, yanked me off the bed, made me get my stuff, and marched me to the front door. The last thing he said before he slammed the door in my face was that I wasn't welcome in their home again."

"Aw, shit." Micah couldn't entirely empathize with what his dad had gone through, because he'd never cared that deeply about someone, but he guessed it had to have hurt him to the core.

Dad snorted. "Oh, believe me, that was just the start. By the time I got home, he'd already called my parents. I guess I found out that night what my father really thought about… homosexuals. Although it might have been better if he'd used *that* term, instead of the one he ultimately chose. He shoved me down onto a chair at the dining table, then sat facing me, his face like thunder." He shivered. "I saw him in a completely different light that night. My mom too. And no, I'm not gonna repeat what they said to me, because it's bad enough that you know they said some stuff. At least now you know why we don't visit them a whole lot." He grimaced. "No way would I subject you to them."

"Was that the end of it?" It certainly went a long way to explaining why he rarely saw his grandparents.

Dad shook his head. "They moved me to a new school, miles away." He scowled. "I was in my final year of high school, getting ready to go to college, and they moved me without so much as a word. I didn't get a say.

On top of that, I wasn't to call Hayden, to try to see him… basically, I wasn't to go within sight of him. And I tried, believe me." He took another drink. "That was when my dad dropped his bombshell. He'd gotten a new job, in Wyoming, and we were moving."

Micah gaped. "He… he didn't move, just to keep you and Hayden apart, did he? Tell me it was just a coincidence that a better job turned up right then." He didn't want to think that his granddad could do something so… cold, so calculating.

Dad shrugged. "To be honest? I have no idea. I wrote letters to Hayden, telling him what was gonna happen. I had no clue if he received them." He swallowed. "I never heard from him again. Later that year, I found out why. I got in touch with a classmate from my old high school. Seems Hayden had moved too. She had no idea where, though."

"Oh, Dad." Micah could feel the misery pouring out of him. "Then what?"

"What do you think? I went to college. Only, instead of going to a college in another state, like I'd planned, my parents insisted I went to the University of Wyoming, and that I stayed at home. I guess they didn't trust me to be out of their sight for too long. And then during the third semester, I met someone." He smiled, and the change in his demeanor was enough to tell Micah who that someone was.

"You met Mom, didn't you?"

Dad nodded. "She was so quiet. A shy little mouse of a girl, in my Economics class."

Micah snickered. "Mom—quiet?"

Dad laughed softly. "Yeah, I know. She changed a lot over the years. For the better, I think. But you should've seen my parents' faces, the night I brought her home to meet them."

"Did... did you ever tell Mom about... Hayden?"

Dad sighed. "You know what? I think I've talked enough for one night. I'm gonna go up to bed, and so should you."

"Oh. Okay." Micah didn't want to go to bed. He wanted to hear more.

"But I promise, this conversation isn't over. We will talk about this again, okay? Just... not in the middle of the night. And not when your sister is around. This is between you and me, all right?"

"All right." Micah got up from the couch. "There *is* one thing, though..."

Dad stood up too. "Yeah? What's that?"

"Paying Greg's hospital bills. Inviting him to stay here. Why?"

Dad picked up the letter and photos, gazing at them. "Good question. I'm not really sure of the answer. I suppose... I'm doing it for Hayden." He raised his head and smiled. "That will have to do for the moment."

"Fair enough." Micah walked slowly toward the door. "I'll see you in a few hours. I'm coming with you to the hospital to see Greg."

Dad joined him. "I never expected anything less. Now get some sleep." Dad surprised him by leaning over and kissing his cheek. "Love you, son."

Micah's chest tightened. "I love you too." He opened the door, and climbed the stairs to his room, the warm drink forgotten. He had a feeling sleep would be a long time coming.

Chapter Four

Greg could still hear them, their mocking laughter as their boots connected with his flesh, the pain that had flared and spread throughout his body. He could still feel their spittle running down his face. He could still see their faces as they leaned over him, jeering and whooping with triumph. Then blissfully, his world had turned black.

He shivered, and reached for his glass of water, as if drinking its coolness would somehow banish those thoughts that tormented him. His leg, swathed in bandages, was a visible reminder. Greg's chest tightened at the memory of his interview with the detectives. He knew deep down he should have told them everything, but he just… couldn't. He'd given them as many details as he could recall about his attackers' appearance, but they didn't seem to hold out much hope that the two men would ever be found. The fact that they'd found his backpack had been nothing short of a miracle. Greg had never expected to see it again, and to find his precious box wasn't lost forever had been…

Wonderful.

Not that he could open it just yet. That would be like finally admitting that Dad was gone. Never coming back.

Greg wanted to hold on a little longer before he caved to his curiosity.

He glanced at the clock on the wall. Visiting hours would be over by eight, and that left him with a little more than two hours remaining. Micah and his father had apparently stayed with him all night, and although they'd promised to return, Greg would understand if they changed their mind. After all, they didn't know him.

What are the odds on Micah being the one to find me? That he'd spotted Greg at all had been further proof of miracles. When they'd tossed Greg out of the car, he'd been dimly aware of the emptiness and desolation of his surroundings. The night was already falling, and no headlights pierced the darkness in which he lay. He could recall trying to crawl toward the road, inching painfully through the snow, until his freezing fingers met the road's surface. Then he'd passed out. But for Micah to not only see him, stop, and bring him to the hospital, but also to be the son of the very man Greg was seeking?

This had to be more than mere coincidence. It was almost—but not quite—enough to make Greg believe that Someone was watching out for him.

Except where was He before that? Greg shivered.

The arrival of the detectives had filled him with dread. They'd wanted to know why Greg had ended up in such a state, and he did *not* want to share that information. At least if his attackers were never caught, his shame would die along with the unsolved case. No one would ever know.

Which was just how Greg wanted it.

When he caught the sound of familiar voices coming from the hallway, Greg was surprised by his body's own reaction. His spirits lifted, and he was suddenly more awake.

They did come back after all. It looked like Micah and his dad were good people.

Micah had to admit, Greg looked brighter than the last time they'd seen him. His face lit up when Dad handed over four or five paperbacks.

"Aw, thanks. Oh wow. You've picked some of my favorites too."

Dad perched on the edge of his bed, carefully avoiding getting near Greg's bandaged leg. "Really? Which ones?" Greg held up Murder On The Orient

Express and Sleeping Murder, and Dad grinned. "Oh, now you *know* I have to ask this. Who is the better detective—Poirot or Miss Marple?"

Greg groaned. "No, you *really* didn't need to ask that."

Micah laughed. "Welcome to my world. Dad had me reading these as soon as I was old enough. And this is a heated topic of debate in our house, trust me."

Greg smiled at Dad. "You remind me of my dad. He loves—*loved*—Agatha Christie too. I spent a lot of time reading to him these past few months."

Dad's smile faltered. "Oh wow. Nice to know some things didn't change." When Greg regarded him inquiringly, Dad sighed. "Who do you think got me into reading them? I was fourteen at the time, and Hayden lent me a copy of The Murder of Roger Ackroyd."

Greg's eyes widened. "You... you knew my dad when you were fourteen?"

Dad nodded. "We sat next to each other in Kindergarten. We played together with our toy cars. We even pretended to be Jedi knights: we both badgered our parents for light sabers for Christmas one year."

Micah gaped. "You... played at being a Jedi?"

"They did toy light sabers back then?" Greg appeared equally incredulous.

"Hey!" Dad said indignantly. "When do you think they first came out? We had to have been... I don't know, maybe six, seven at the time? And it was a yellow inflatable blade, attached to a flashlight. The only problem was, we got a little... vigorous in our playing."

"What happened?" Micah thought he knew his Dad: this was nothing short of astounding.

Dad gave them a sheepish smile. "They sprung a

leak and deflated." Both Micah and Greg laughed at that. "Fortunately, the manufacturers included a patch kit for repairing them."

Greg shook his head. "I'm still trying to get my head around you and my dad, playing Star Wars." His eyes twinkled. "Which one of you was Darth Vader?"

Dad scowled. "Me, just because I was taller. The number of times I begged him to switch, so I could get to be Obi Wan Kenobi, but *no.*" Then his face took on a faraway expression. "Happy times."

Except now Micah knew the extent of their relationship, he had an idea of how bittersweet those happy memories had to be.

Dad straightened. "So, have the doctors seen you today?"

Greg nodded. "They told me it could have been much worse." He gestured toward his face. "I know this is a mess—I had the nurse bring me a mirror—but apparently I was lucky not to have internal bleeding and injuries. I've got a lump on the back of my head. My belly is quite spectacular, now all the bruising is coming out there too. As for my leg, the doc said it's a stable fracture of the femur shaft. They've put a pin in it, and there's a plate attached to the bone."

"How long before you'll be up and about?" Micah asked.

"I could be mobile—with crutches—in about three weeks, if I rest up and let it heal. In the meantime, I'll have a cast to keep me from moving my knee. I guess they just want to keep me from putting pressure on the bone. But I won't be driving this side of Christmas."

"The doc said something about physical therapy?"

"Yes, sir. They're going to teach me some exercises to do." Greg bit his lip. "Were… were you serious about me staying with you when they discharge me?"

Dad arched his eyebrows. "Of *course* I was serious. You think we're gonna let you head back to— where is it you live, anyhow?"

Greg's face took on a guarded look. "My mom and stepdad live in San Diego."

Micah didn't miss the wording of Greg's response. "Don't you live with them?" Judging from Greg's careful expression, he guessed it was a question Greg wasn't all that keen to answer.

Dad dove right in. "That settles it. I'm not letting you go all the way to southern California, not with a busted leg. Besides, we're almost at Thanksgiving. Granted, it might not be the kind of Thanksgiving you're used to at home—you'll get several feet of snow, for one thing, and it can get as low as maybe minus ten degrees, as opposed to a whole lotta sunshine and a tad warmer in San Diego." Then he smiled. "The plus side is that *you* won't have to lift a finger. *You* will be sitting in a comfy chair, with that leg up, snuggled under a warm blanket, while *we* run around like headless chickens." He glanced at Micah. "We haven't exactly gotten the hang of cooking Thanksgiving dinner yet, have we, son?"

Greg seemed perplexed by this. "I… don't understand."

Micah came around to the other side of his bed and pulled up the chair. He removed his jacket and scarf, before sitting down. "My mom was the one who was always in charge, but… we lost her a couple of years ago." If he closed his eyes right then, he could still see her in the kitchen, stuffing the turkey and watching him and Naomi as they prepared the vegetables, Dad safely out of the way where she couldn't give him something to do. More importantly, where he couldn't get into trouble: Dad was a menace in the kitchen.

I guess he's had to learn a lot these past two years. Micah's sense of loss hadn't diminished all that much: it still felt like a knife in his gut.

Greg's breathing hitched. "I'm so sorry. Then is it just you and your dad?"

"There's my sister, Naomi. She's nineteen, pre-med." Micah attempted a half-smile. "And a major pain in the ass."

Greg laughed quietly. "Isn't that a prerequisite of little sisters?" Both Micah and his dad joined him in his laughter.

When Dad stopped laughing, he looked Greg up and down. "The police have taken your statement then?"

"Yes, sir."

"So what happened? Do you know who did this?" Micah couldn't believe there had only been one attacker: Greg might be on the skinny side, but surely he'd have made an effort to fight off one guy. There was too much damage for that.

Greg's face kind of... closed in. "I'd never seen them before." He cleared his throat. "What is Wright like? I got the impression it's a little on the small side."

Micah got the message, loud and clear. Greg did *not* want to talk about what had happened to him, which only made Micah more curious. There had to be more to this incident than a random robbery. Dad was right—the extent of Greg's injuries spoke of malice.

Dad snickered. "Small? I guess that's a fair

assessment. Mind, we have everything you could possibly want. Hell, we even have our own Subway now!" He cackled. "There's a supermarket that sells just about anything, a library, a fire station, not to mention two gas stations." He counted off on his fingers. "Then there's the hotel, the steakhouse, and of course, happy hour food at Hanks."

Greg smiled. "What more could you ask for?"

"Course, we also have three churches. Yep, all denominations are catered for, including the Mormons. Hell, you can even have a manicure at the Rusty Nail."

"I'll have to remember that." Greg's face clouded over. "Not sure I'll be paying any of the churches a visit, however."

"Son, you can do whatever you want, all right?" Dad coughed. "And once you're hobbling around, maybe Micah will take you out for a spin around Wright."

Micah snorted. "Sure. That'll take all of five minutes." He grinned at Greg. "What my dad doesn't tell you, is that for everything Wright *doesn't* have? There's Gillette, about forty-five minutes north of there. That would make for a more interesting trip."

Greg smiled. "Then I guess I'd better get healed up pretty quickly." His eyes widened. "Oh. The doctor said there's an information sheet I'm going to need, all about what to do once I'm discharged. Maybe you need a copy, if I'm going to be staying with you."

To Micah's surprise, Dad grasped Greg's hand in his. "Not if—*when*. And you can stay as long as you've a mind to. I'm not about to show you the door, once you're up on crutches. Unless there's something in California that you urgently need to get back to?"

Greg swallowed. "No, sir. Nothing urgent."

Dad nodded and released his hand. "Then we're gonna leave you to your reading. Not to mention some sleeping. Sleep's good for you."

Micah took the hint. He stood, wrapped his thick scarf around his neck and pulled on his jacket. "I'll come by tomorrow, see how you're doing."

Greg frowned. "Really, you mustn't put yourself out. I'm sure you must have much more important things to do than visit me."

Micah smiled. "It's not an imposition, honest." If it were him in that hospital bed, he'd be climbing the walls within a day or so. He walked around the bed to join Dad. "Happy reading."

"Wait." Greg stretched out a hand toward him. Micah stared at it for a moment, then clasped it. Greg took a breath. "Thank you. You saved my life."

Micah smiled. "You already thanked me this morning, remember?"

"I know, but that was before I realized just how close I came to…" Greg took another shaky breath and addressed Dad. "Do you think we could talk sometime, about… my dad? Once I'm out of here?"

Dad's face lit up. "Sure. I'd like that." He coughed. "Come on, son. Naomi will be foaming at the mouth if we get home and dinner is ruined."

Micah rolled his eyes. "Then we'll go out to eat." He winked at Greg. "It'll taste better than her cooking anyhow." He gave Greg a final nod, then followed his dad out of the room.

"He looks brighter," Dad commented as they walked along the hallway. "But we'd better give some thought to where he's gonna sleep. Can't have him going up and down stairs all the time, not on that leg. And he'll need a bed that's not too high, one he can easily get in and out of."

"There's the sofa bed in my room. It's nice and low. And if he feels awkward about being in my room, we can move it someplace else. Let's face it, we got plenty of room." Dad had built onto the original house, but now that it was just the three of them, sometimes they rattled around in there like bbs in a bucket.

"True, but I'm thinking the guest bedroom might be a better fit, instead of your room. Can't see him coping well with the stairs." Dad stopped at the elevator. "Ya know, the more time we spend with him, the more I can see the resemblance. Especially around the eyes." He sighed. "Hayden had the most amazing eyes." The elevator arrived, and they stepped inside.

Micah studied his dad in silence. He had so many questions, but the timing didn't feel right.

Maybe once Greg is staying with us, Dad will open up a little.

He wanted to know more about his dad's first love. More importantly, Micah wanted to know if his mom had known about it.

Chapter Five

"You look happy," Micah commented as he entered the hospital room.

Greg raised his eyes heavenward. "You have *no* idea. They let me take a shower this morning."

He laughed. "Wow. How… exciting."

Greg speared him with a look. "*You* try having a nurse give you sponge baths for almost a week, and see how *you* like it."

Micah chuckled. "How did you manage with that?" He pointed to the leg cast that encased most of

Greg's left leg, stiff and black, with Velcro fastenings.

"They covered it with plastic. I still had to sit on a stool in the shower, but oh my *God*, the sheer joy of being able to wash myself—alone."

"You can use my bathroom while you're staying with us." Micah smiled. "It's a walk-in shower. No bath to climb in and out of. Plus, there's another on the first floor."

"Oh, that sounds great." Greg grinned. "And now for the good news. They're discharging me today."

Micah beamed. The doctors had mentioned this the previous day, but everything had depended on Greg's latest examination. "Excellent. I'll call Dad and let him know we're good to go."

Greg pointed to the chair next to the window, where two shiny crutches leaned against it. "Look what I got." His eyes widened. "Oh. I forgot. The physical therapist came by earlier. She said someone's going to come out to your house to work with me. I don't have to travel anyplace."

"That's great!"

Greg nodded, smiling widely. "Apparently, they'll contact you, to make arrangements and put together a schedule. And she says I need to spend as much time as I can, getting around on the crutches. She said immobility is not healthy. She also said not to overdo it." He snickered. "What she actually said was, not to be signing up to run in any 400-yard sprints just yet."

Micah laughed. "Yeah, well, we'll be there to keep an eye on you."

"How's the painting been this week?" Greg fixed him with a hard stare. "You *have* been painting, right? I mean, you've not been spending all your time getting things ready for when I arrive, right?"

Micah was starting to regret telling Greg about his work. "You're worse than my dad, do you know that?" Not that he really minded. Greg had appeared genuinely interested in Micah's paintings, and when Micah had brought along photos of some of his completed work, Greg had been speechless with admiration. What amazed him was how quickly a rapport had been established between them.

Greg chuckled. "Well, maybe someone needs to keep an eye on *you.*"

"You volunteering for the job?" Micah joked.

Greg laughed. "It's not like I'll have much to do, right? I can crack a whip, if that's what's required."

Micah arched his eyebrows. "Kinky."

Greg snorted. "Doof."

Micah's gaze alighted on the wooden box on top of the cabinet beside the bed. It was still wrapped in plastic.

"That was my Dad's." Greg's voice was quiet. "He left a note saying he wanted me to have it."

"But you haven't opened it." Micah didn't know how Greg could stand it. Curiosity would have been eating Micah alive by now.

Greg let out a soft sigh. "I know. I will, just… not yet." He regarded Micah closely. "I love how you and your dad get along. You have this really great relationship."

"Didn't you get along with your dad?"

Greg shrugged. "I didn't really know him all that well. He and Mom split up when I was little, and he wasn't around when I was growing up. It was only once I got to college that I decided to get to know him. I wanted to know more, like why they split up in the first place."

"And did you find out?"

"Not really." Greg's face clouded over. "All he would say, was that he had to stop living a lie. Mom wouldn't talk about it either. But then, by that time, she'd met Damon Chambers."

"Your stepdad?"

Greg nodded. "He's okay, I guess. I mean, he wanted me to take his name, for us to be a family, but…." He swallowed. "Would you mind if we don't continue this conversation?"

"As long as we get to finish it eventually." Micah hated that Greg was hurting.

"Sure. We're going to have lots of time for talking, right?" He smiled. "It's not like I'll be going anywhere for a while." Greg straightened. "So. How about I put all my stuff together, and we see if they'll let me out of this place?"

Micah nodded. "That sounds like a plan, except how about you stay put and *I* pack your things? Then I'll go find a nurse. I'll move the car too, so that you don't have far to hobble once you get outside."

"Outside." Greg's face lit up. "Fresh air. Edible food."

Micah snorted. "I'd hold off on those kinda comments until you've tasted my dad's cooking."

"Can your sister cook? Or you? What about you?" Greg gazed at him hopefully.

Micah laughed. "Naomi can cook pasta, and that's about it. I swear that's all she eats when she's in school. Me? My specialty is pizza."

"Making it from scratch?"

Micah snickered. "Nah—shoving a frozen one into the oven."

Greg narrowed his gaze. "Hmm. I'm suddenly rethinking this whole, 'go-and-stay-with-Micah' deal. Because... malnutrition?" He grinned. "Should I be worried here?"

Micah opened his eyes wide. "I may have exaggerated a little about my dad's cooking. It *is* edible. Well, just about." He looked around for Greg's backpack, and spied it on the chair. "Let's get you packed up so we can spring you from prison." He gave a furtive glance over his shoulder. "Just don't let the nurse hear me say that." For some reason, Micah was excited by the prospect of taking Greg home. The past five days had been good. He'd visited every day, often spending three or more hours with Greg. But the conversation about his mom and stepdad was the most personal Greg had gotten in that whole time.

Maybe he'll feel freer to talk about himself once we're out of here.

Micah hoped so, because he still had a lot of questions to ask.

Greg gazed out at the passing scenery from the back seat. "There's not a whole lot out here, is there?"

Micah chuckled. "This is Highway 59, heading toward Gillette, but we hit Wright first. And no, there's not much to see."

Greg couldn't see a thing: everywhere was covered with a deep blanket of snow. "Is it more interesting without the snow?"

Micah laughed. "Not really." He inclined his head in a northeasterly direction. "Over there is Thunder Basin National Grassland. It has some great views of the Rocky Mountains, but mostly it's just flat. That's where I was coming from when I found you."

Greg looked out at the snow and shivered. "Thank God you did." His leg was aching. "How long does it take to get to Wright?"

"About seventy-five minutes from the hospital, give or take. We're not that far now."

Greg stared at the landscape. "I think… I was coming from the other direction." When Micah had first mentioned Gillette, the name had struck a chord. Greg was pretty sure he'd passed through Gillette, and that the truck had dropped him off just south of there.

He wasn't likely to forget Jake's Tavern in a hurry, that was for sure.

"You okay back there?" Micah peered at him in the rear-view mirror. "You went quiet all of a sudden. Is your leg bothering you?"

"A little." He had a bag full of pills for the pain, only he wasn't that keen on taking them.

"Well, when we get you home, you can take your meds. Remember, the nurse said you can take two every four hours. When did you last take some?"

"Just before you arrived," Greg said absently. He wasn't thinking about pills—he was recalling a cute guy with dark eyes and a nice line. *I guess it just goes to prove you really can't judge a book by its cover.* That pleasant exterior had hidden a whole lot of ugliness.

"No wonder you're hurting. Do you want to take them now? I've got a bottle of water here."

Greg told himself for what had to be the hundredth time how damn lucky he'd been that night. Micah was one of the good guys. "Actually? Yeah." He opened his backpack where it sat on the foot mat, rummaging inside it until he found the bag full of pain meds. Micah reached back to hand him the bottle. Greg pressed out two of the capsules and chased them down with a good gulp of cold water. "Thanks." He held out the bottle.

"You keep it. I've got another here." Micah pointed to the side of the road. "That's where I found you, by the way."

Greg jerked up his head and stared at the white landscape. There was nothing to see but snow, miles from anywhere. *Those bastards.* A shudder rippled through him.

"Hey." Micah's gaze met his in the mirror. "You're all right. You made it."

"Because of you." Greg took a couple of calming breaths, expelling his tension along with the sick feeling in the pit of his stomach. Seeing where they'd dumped him only served to make their intentions clear. Then something deep in his belly turned over. *What if... what if I wasn't the only one? What if... they've done this before?* Hot bile rose up in his throat, and he gagged.

"Greg?" The car veered over to the side of the road and came to a stop. Greg had barely enough time to open the car door before he threw up onto the snow.

Micah unfastened his seat belt, twisted around, and leaned between the seats. "Are you okay?"

The cold air hit Greg's face and he shivered, wiping his mouth with the back of his hand.

"Here." Micah yanked open the glove box, before thrusting a couple of sheets of paper towel into his hand. Greg took them gratefully, wiping away the last traces of vomit from his face and hand. He balled up the towel, looking for somewhere to put it.

"You might as well throw it out there. It's biodegradable anyway." Micah gazed at him closely. "Do you get car sick?"

"No, not usually," Greg replied truthfully. It wasn't like he could tell Micah what was in his thoughts. He could only pray he was wrong. Because if there was the slightest possibility that he was correct.... Another shiver coursed through his body, and he pulled the car door shut.

Micah frowned. "I'm getting you home as fast as I can. Dad will have the fire lit, and the house will be warm."

Right then, Greg doubted he'd ever be warm again. His fears seeped into his bones, spreading ice through his veins.

Please, God, let me be wrong.

By the time Micah switched off the engine, Dad was already out of the house and walking toward the car. Micah noticed instantly that he'd cleared a path to the front door.

"It's a nice-looking house," Greg commented.

Before Micah could respond, Dad opened the back door, and then crouched down next to Greg. "Here's how we're gonna do this. Once you're out of the car, I'm going to carry you into the house, all right?"

"I have crutches," Greg protested. "I'm sure I can manage."

Dad scowled. "The ground is too icy for crutches. And you're gonna be staying in the downstairs guest room, because no *way* am I letting you climb the stairs. You can tackle that particular hurdle in a few weeks, but not now. And let's be honest here. You probably don't weigh more than a hundred pounds, even with that cast."

Greg glared at him. "I know I'm skinny, but *Jesus!*"

Micah snickered. "It's much easier if you don't argue with him, really." Greg grumbled, but Dad was ignoring him, already helping him out of the car. Then he lifted Greg like he weighed nothing, his left arm supporting Greg's leg. Micah pulled Greg's backpack from the car, along with his crutches, and followed them to the house, his dad walking carefully over the newly revealed paved path. Micah pushed open the door and Dad turned sideways to enter, making sure to keep Greg's leg away from the walls. Greg had his arms around Dad's neck.

Dad carried him through into the living room, where the fire was already blazing, spreading its heat to every corner. He eased Greg down onto the couch in front of it. "Welcome to our home. I thought we'd give you a while to get warm, then we'll have lunch. *Then* you can see your room."

Greg nodded, his gaze traveling around the room.

"This is great. Really cozy. And I love the fire." He turned to Micah. "Where do you paint? Is your studio on this floor? Can I see it?"

Micah laughed. "You've just gotten through the door. Take a breath, for God's sake." He peered at his dad. "What's for lunch?"

"Soup. I figured that was easiest. And I just made some bread."

Greg let out a low whistle. "You make your own bread?" He stared at Micah. "I thought you said he couldn't cook?"

Dad gave Micah a hard stare. "Oh, he did, did he?" His lips twitched.

Micah snorted. "Hey, don't go giving him a false impression. Anyone can switch on a bread machine and measure out ingredients."

Greg glanced from Micah, to Dad, whose face flushed, then back to Micah, before bursting into laughter.

Dad huffed. "Okay, so maybe I'm not the World's Best Cook."

Micah went over to him and gave him a hug. "Maybe not, but I think you're a serious contender for the World's Best Dad." Dad's faced glowed, but he said nothing, opting instead to return Micah's hug.

"I'll go fix lunch." Dad disappeared into the kitchen.

Greg leaned back against the cushions. "So what's the layout of this floor? Seeing as this is where I'm going to be located for a while."

"First things first." Micah grabbed the old coffee table that Dad had brought in from the garage. He placed it at a right angle to the couch, then covered it with a couple of pillows. "This is for your leg. We figured it was the right height." He helped Greg to sit properly, lifting his leg carefully onto the pillows. "How's that?"

"Perfect," Greg said with a sigh. "And I think the meds have just kicked in. I'm feeling kind of muzzy."

"Then you just sit there and be muzzy," Micah said with a smile. "You don't have any place to be, and nothing to do but heal. And if you want to take a nap after lunch, that's fine. Like Dad said, sleep is good." When Greg didn't respond, Micah peered closely at him.

Greg had fallen asleep.

Micah crept out of the room and into the kitchen. *He can eat when he wakes up.*

Chapter Six

Greg was comfortable, pleasantly full, and content for the first time in a long while. The day seemed to have gone by so slowly, and yet that wasn't a bad thing at all. He'd dozed on the couch, chatted with Micah, looked through photo albums that Micah's dad had left beside him, and eaten plenty. His appetite had finally returned, and despite Micah's jokes about their cooking prowess, he and his dad had prepared a great meal.

It was almost enough to banish Greg's fears. Almost—but not quite.

By the time nine o'clock rolled around, it was obvious Micah's ass was dragging. His dad noticed too, and told him to go to bed. It was only once Micah had left them that his dad told Greg that Micah had been up since the crack of dawn, working on a canvas, before coming to collect Greg from the hospital.

"And before you start feeling guilty," his Dad interjected, "he usually gets up early to paint. He says the light is better. Micah hates to paint by artificial light. Says the colors don't appear the same in light that isn't natural." He smiled. "Not that there's a whole lotta light early in the morning at this time of the year. But yeah, he's not a night owl, that boy." He peered at Greg. "And what about you? Are you a dawn or dusk guy?"

"I guess I'm more of a morning person," Greg admitted. He sighed. "I can't thank you enough, sir. This is really kind of you."

"Hush. Like I said last weekend, you're Hayden's kid. There isn't much I wouldn't do for ya." He cleared his throat. "Greg, I like your manners, honest, but… do you think you could call me Joshua? Sir kinda reminds me of my dad, and trust me, that's not a good thing."

Greg blinked. "Okay… I guess. It feels a little weird, I have to admit." Then he thought about it. Micah's da—*Joshua*—had been friends with his own dad. Maybe a little familiarity was okay in those circumstances. But that thought led him off down an avenue full of questions. "Do you think… could we talk a bit about my dad?" Top of Greg's list was that letter. What on earth could his dad have written that would make a grown man weep the way Joshua had done? And what was so all-fired important that Dad had wanted to share with Joshua?

Joshua stilled. "I suppose we should, really. Unless... you'd rather wait until tomorrow? After a good night's sleep, I mean."

Greg knew evasion when he heard it, and *Strike while the iron is hot* was one of his mom's favorite sayings. "I didn't know my dad all that well. It was only during the past couple of years that we... reconnected."

"How come?" Joshua sat beside him on the couch. "What happened between you two?"

"Nothing. But he and mom split up when I was little." Greg paused, uncertain as to whether he should continue. The opportunity seemed too good to waste. "What I've never discovered is the reason why. Mom says nothing about it. All my dad would say was that he wanted to stop living a lie, and I don't know what he meant by that. Oh, I've come up with so many theories, but..." He stared at his clasped hands, lost in his own thoughts.

Joshua's breathing hitched, and Greg glanced up sharply. "What if... what if *I* knew why?"

Greg's heartbeat sped up. "You... *you* do?"

Joshua regarded him in silence for a moment, then got up from the couch and left the room. Greg stared after him in bewilderment, until Joshua returned, carrying the envelope Greg had delivered. He removed the letter and something else, that he handed to Greg. "This is your dad and me, when we were seventeen."

Greg gazed at the photos, unable to hold back a smile when he saw the goofball expressions on his dad's and Joshua's face. "Looks like you two had a few laughs."

"God, we did."

Then Greg studied the final two images, and it

was as if a hand tightened around his chest. That look… almost naked emotion, so plain to see that…

Slowly Greg raised his head to meet Joshua's gaze. "Is there something you want to tell me?"

Joshua sighed. "I think I'll let your dad do that." And with that, he handed Greg the letter.

Greg's hand trembled as he held the sheets, covered in a familiar scrawl.

Jackson, WY
April 29, 2017

Joshua,

I know I've probably left this too late, but…

You have no idea how many times I've thought about trying to find you these last few years. I told myself you were happy, that you had your own life… that you didn't need me waltzing into it and raking up the past. But then two things happened that made me rethink that decision.

I'm so sorry about your wife, Joshua. I saw her obituary in the paper. It said you were married for twenty-four years, and that you have two children. Then I saw where you live. My God. We've been living in the same state for the past twenty years or so, and we never knew.

I hope you had a good life with her. You deserve that.

Yet knowing how close we are? Hell, I could get in my car and drive non-stop for just over nine hours, and I'd be on your doorstep. Not that I will. I still can't find the courage to come visit you. Too much time has passed.

A CHRISTMAS PROMISE

And now… I'm writing this letter, knowing I'll never mail it to you, because to do that would be like admitting that I'll never see you again. That would be like giving in to the cancer that's consuming me.

Cancer. Yes. I've got anywhere between three and six months, they tell me. No surgery—I'm beyond that. Beyond chemotherapy and radiation too. The ironic thing is I never even realized I was so ill. This bastard snuck up on me, and by the time I got the diagnosis, it was already too late to do a damn thing about it.

So little time…

I have to get down on paper what I wish I could say to you in person. It's as close as I'm going to get, so here goes…

I loved you. God, how I loved you. Joshua, my sweet boy, my first—my only—true love. I've never forgotten you. Not for one single minute. I got married too, but unlike you, I couldn't stick at it. Something deep inside of me knew it was wrong, that I only married Debra to please my parents—that I never loved her, at least not the way I loved you. I have a son too. Greg. After years apart, we're finally building the kind of relationship a father and son should have, only it's too little, too late. My hope for him is that he finds someone who loves him half as much as I loved you.

I should have tried to find you sooner, I know that now. But as time went by, I made more and more excuses.

Remember me, Joshua. Remember what we shared. I look at how the world is changing, and part of me likes to imagine that we could have had what others now enjoy—marriage, equality…. Happiness.

Never forget I loved you first.

Hayden

Greg's vision blurred, and tears dripped onto the paper. He knew he was crying for so many reasons; the father he'd only gotten to know a little of: the love that permeated those few lines: the knowledge that he and his dad were more alike than either of them had guessed; and finally, the heartache Joshua and his dad had clearly suffered.

A gentle hand covered his. "Here." A folded cotton handkerchief was pressed into his palm.

Greg wiped his eyes and looked up. "What happened? Did you break up or something?"

Joshua swallowed. "Our parents. That's what happened. Then my family moved from Alabama to Wyoming. I had no idea where Hayden ended up—now that I know about you, I'm assuming California. I never heard from him again."

Greg nodded. "So you and he... my dad was... gay?"

"Gay, bi, I'm not certain. I can only speak for myself."

"And... did you feel for him, the way he felt for you?"

"God, yes." Joshua's eyes glistened, and Greg cursed the fact that he couldn't move the way he wanted. Joshua shifted closer and held his arms wide.

That was all the invitation Greg needed.

He buried his face in Joshua's chest, and the dam burst. Hot tears soaked into Joshua's thick shirt, and Greg made no attempt to rein them in. Joshua's body shuddered, and Greg knew he too was crying. Little by little, he regained his composure, until finally his tears dried up and he pulled away, exhausted.

Joshua pushed Greg's hair back from his forehead. "You okay?" His eyes were red, his cheeks blotchy.

Greg nodded, inhaling deeply. "Sorry about that."

Joshua sniffed. "Nothing to be sorry for. And there was I, thinking I was all cried out."

A thought occurred to him. "Does Micah know? Has he read this?" Greg handed the sheets and photos to Joshua.

"He knows, but… you're the only other person to read it." Joshua gazed at him thoughtfully. "If your dad was never going to mail this, what changed his mind?"

Greg sagged against the seat cushions. "The first thing I knew about the letter was the day before he died. He gave me the envelope and made me promise to mail it to you. I was to make sure you received it."

Joshua sat so still. "Did… did he suffer, at the end?"

Greg couldn't look at him, couldn't stand to see the pain in his eyes. "He was heavily sedated. He kept pointing to the nightstand drawer, so I opened it. I found the envelope." It had made Greg's heart ache, just hearing his dad trying to get the words out. But finally, Greg had grasped what he wanted. "When he'd… gone, I looked you up and found your address. I wrote it on a slip of paper and put it in my wallet. I was going to mail it, honestly. But then I got to thinking… It was my dad's final request. The least I could do would be to deliver it in person."

"Not that you weren't in the least bit curious," Joshua said with a wry smile.

Heat crawled up Greg's chest and neck, finally reaching his ears that he felt sure were glowing, they were so hot. "Possibly," he admitted.

Joshua folded the letter and replaced it in the envelope, adding the strip of photos.

"Were they in with the letter?"

Joshua shook his head. "I kept these. They were the only photos of him that I had."

Greg stilled. "Did…. Did your wife ever see them?" Joshua nodded. "Did she say anything?" Greg doubted anyone could miss the almost tangible, emotional connection between the two young men in that last photo. Not unless they deliberately chose to ignore it…

Joshua glanced at the clock above the fireplace. "I think that's a tale for another night. It's getting late, you've had a long day, and you need to rest." Greg opened his mouth to protest that he wasn't tired, and a yawn escaped. Joshua smiled. "I rest my case."

"You promise you'll tell me the rest of the story?" Greg had more questions, but they had time.

"I will. I'll tell both of you."

That was good enough for Greg. Then Joshua slipped his arms under Greg's back and leg, and lifted him carefully into the air. "Bedtime."

Greg clung on as Joshua carried him to the guest bedroom that would be his for a while. How long for, Greg had no idea. Long enough for him to find out more about his dad, and the man who had loved him.

Joshua set him down on the bed. "I'll wish you a good night, then."

"Wait!" When Joshua halted, Greg found the words he'd wanted to say since Joshua had carried him through the front door. "I've been meaning to thank you for paying my hospital bills. You didn't need to do that. Only, now I kind of understand why you did." He lifted his chin and met Joshua's gaze. "That was because of my dad, right?"

Joshua nodded. "Like I said… anything for Hayden's boy." He gave Greg a warm smile. "Now get some sleep." He left the room, closing the door quietly behind him.

Almost in slow motion, Greg undressed, removing the sweat pants that Micah had brought for him. He supposed he'd get used to the cast, but it frustrated the hell out of him, and he couldn't wait for it to be removed for good. He lay in bed, his mind going over his dad's letter.

Greg's last thought before sleep overtook him was one of regret.

I should have told him I was gay. I thought we had more time.

Chapter Seven

Greg had no idea what had awoken him, and for a moment he had no clue where he was. Then he heard the light tap on his door, and everything came flooding back.

Micah's home. Joshua and my dad… in love.

It still felt unreal.

"Greg? You awake?"

Greg rubbed his eyes. "Sure. Come in."

The door opened, and Micah came in carrying a mug, steam rising from it. "Hey. Good morning. How did you sleep? I brought you some coffee." He grinned. "It's better than the hospital version, I swear."

Greg stuffed a pillow behind him and sat up. "That wouldn't be difficult." He sniffed at the T-shirt he'd slept in. "You think I could do some laundry today?" He'd packed light for the trip, but he'd already run out of clean clothing.

"Yeah, sure." Micah placed the mug on the nightstand, then perched on the edge of the bed. "So how did you sleep?"

"Like a log." His leg had bothered him some, and there had been more than enough simmering inside his head to keep sleep at bay, but once he'd taken his meds, that was it, lights out. He was still feeling pretty zonked. "But I think those pills are really strong."

Micah arched his eyebrows. "They're probably standard painkillers, but being as slight as you are? Yeah, I can see how they'd knock you out." He gazed at the cast. "Is that comfortable?"

"I don't think it's supposed to be comfortable, but it does its job." Speaking of which… "I guess I'd better get into a routine of changing the bandages. The hospital gave me instructions."

"Do the pins have to be taken out at some point?"

Greg shook his head. "I just have to make sure I tell people, you know, like when I go through airport security and stuff like that. And my dentist needs to know, apparently."

"I was thinking about you this morning when I woke up." Micah's brow furrowed. "You don't have a phone, do you?"

"No. That was taken, along with my wallet."

Except Greg had a sneaking suspicion that had been to give the illusion of a robbery.

"So… you don't know if people have been trying to contact you." Micah gazed at him steadily. "Like your family. Do they even know where you are? Did you call them while you were in hospital?"

Shit. Micah's question brought him face to face with the reality he'd been trying so hard to avoid. "No, I didn't."

Micah's eyes widened. "Aw, Greg. Don't you think you should have? I mean, they might be worried sick."

"I doubt that, somehow." He couldn't keep the bitterness from pervading his words. Maybe he had them all wrong, but then again….

Micah kept silent, but his face said plenty. The skin around his mouth tightened, and he frowned.

Maybe Micah had a point. "Look, I promise I'll call them today. If your dad is okay with it."

Micah smiled, his tension clearly dissipating. "He'll be fine with it. Now, I can take your clothes and add them to the laundry, but in the meantime, I've been thinking. That pair of sweats you wore home from the hospital? You can keep those, plus I have a couple of old pairs that would probably fit over that cast. And if they don't, we can always cut off the leg. They'll be warm enough to wear around the house, and it's not like you'll be going anywhere for a while. Plus, I have some sweaters that will probably fit you, and some thick socks. It didn't look like you had all that much clothing with you."

Like Micah and his dad hadn't done enough for

him already. "Thanks. That sounds great. And thanks for the coffee."

Micah got up from the bed. "I'll leave you alone to enjoy it in peace. And if you need a hand getting to the bathroom, give me a yell. It's only a couple of doors away, and it has a shower." He smiled. "I have a roll of plastic wrapping in my studio. I'll bring some to cover your cast." Micah walked over to the door. "There's a robe in the closet for you. Call out when you're ready." He left the room, closing the door gently behind him.

Greg picked up the mug and inhaled the aroma. Ever since Joshua had volunteered to pay Greg's medical bills, the whole situation had taken on a 'too good to be true' dimension. Add to that Micah's hospital visits, a place to stay while he recuperated, the kindness they'd shown him ever since Joshua had carried him into the house….

There are some wonderful people in this world. Greg was pretty sure he was staying with two of them.

"Where's Greg?" Dad removed the pack of bacon from the fridge, along with a carton of eggs.

"In the shower." Micah had left him the plastic wrapping, figuring Greg would be more comfortable doing it himself. He'd helped Greg to the bathroom, stressing that if he got into any difficulty in the shower, he had to call for help. It had to be awkward, dealing with a shower when he couldn't put any weight on his leg. "He looks kinda tired. I think his meds are making him a little fuzzy headed."

"Well, that leg has to be painful." Dad broke six eggs into a glass bowl, then whisked them with a fork.

Micah peered at his dad. "What time did you two get to bed last night?"

"Oh, not that late. We did some talking." Dad put down the fork and leaned against the cabinet. "We both got a little emotional, to be honest. I let him read his dad's letter."

Micah stilled. "Really?"

Dad gave him a sad smile. "Don't worry. I always intended letting you read it, but it seemed important to let Greg read it first. His father and all."

Micah got that, he truly did, but… "There's a lot of stuff you still have to tell me, isn't there?" He didn't like this feeling that Dad was keeping him in the dark. *Since when did we ever keep secrets from each other?*

Dad regarded him in silence, then sighed. "Yeah. And I promise, one day soon, I'll sit you both down and we'll talk. Let Greg get settled in first, okay?"

Micah nodded, slightly mollified. "He needs to call California, by the way. His mom and stepdad don't know what's happened."

Dad gaped. "Seriously? God, Micah. I had no idea. Yeah, he needs to do that first." He cocked his head. "Shower's stopped. Go tell him I'm getting breakfast ready. I assume eggs, bacon and toast will be okay."

Micah left him and went into the little hallway that led to the guest bedroom, bathroom and laundry room. He tapped on the bathroom door. "Dad's cooking breakfast. How do you like your eggs?"

"Scrambled, please. I'll be right out. By the way, this bench in the shower is a godsend."

Micah chuckled. "That was my mom's idea. She planned that bathroom. You managed okay?"

From behind the door, he caught Greg's laugh. "Yeah, I coped just fine. All I had to do was sit here. Your mom liked her showers, didn't she? This one has all the bells and whistles, doesn't it?"

Micah knew what Greg referred to. That shower had a rainfall head set into the ceiling, a couple of handheld shower heads, and finally a set of small jets set into the tiles. Mom loved her creature comforts.

"I won't be long. Just have to unwrap myself first. Then we'll see how long it takes me to hobble to you." Greg snickered.

"If you need a hand, you just yell, okay?" Micah left him to it and rejoined Dad in the kitchen. "Is Naomi not coming home this weekend? I'd have thought she'd want to meet Greg."

Dad sighed. "Apparently, she has a big test on Monday, so she's burying herself in her books. But she'll be here Wednesday."

For a moment, Micah was perplexed, then he remembered. Thanksgiving was only six days away. "I'd better put a grocery list together." He stared at his dad. "You *did* remember to order a turkey, right?"

"No, of course not. I thought we'd have pizza this year." Dad rolled his eyes. "It's being delivered Wednesday morning, oh ye of little faith."

Micah held up his hands defensively. "I'm just saying. I remember last year."

"Hey!" Dad glared at him. "So I forgot. As your

sister is so fond of saying, bite me. And we did have a turkey, didn't we?"

"Yes, we did," Micah said slowly. "It was the last one in the store, and about the size of a pigeon." He pointed to the stove. "Don't you have eggs to cook?"

Dad narrowed his gaze. "God, you remind me of your mother sometimes." Then his face softened. "Thank God."

A muted cough came from the doorway. Greg stood there in soft, dark gray sweats and a dark blue sweater. He gestured to his leg. "Look, no cast," he joked. He hobbled awkwardly into the room, his hands gripping the crutches tightly, his left leg held stiffly off the ground. "Still haven't gotten the hang of these," he said sheepishly.

Dad was at his side in a heartbeat. "You come sit over here," he said, guiding Greg toward a chair. "Micah? Grab some cushions for me, will ya?" He took the crutches from Greg once he'd sat down.

Micah ran into the living room and returned with a couple of cushions, which Dad placed on another chair, before carefully lifting Greg's leg onto it. "You need to rest this leg, all right? Don't go putting any weight on it. And this way, you can keep it straight."

Greg sighed. "I'm not about to fall or anything. And although I appreciate the help, I have to get used to getting around on those things." Then he winced.

"Sure you do." Dad regarded him closely. "And I'm gonna go right on acting like a mother hen until that leg stops hurting as much as it obviously does."

Micah touched Greg's shoulder. "Where are your meds?"

"On the nightstand in my room."

"I'll get them." Without giving Greg the opportunity to reply, Micah left them and went to Greg's room. The sheet of capsules sat next to the wrapped wooden box. Micah picked them up and hurried back to the kitchen. Dad had already poured out a glass of water.

Greg pressed out two capsules and chased them down with the water, his face pale.

"And when breakfast is over, you are gonna sit on the couch and do absolutely nothing for the rest of the day, except read, watch TV, or any other activities that don't require movement. Do I make myself clear?" Dad gave Greg a firm stare.

"Crystal." Greg's stomach rumbled, and he flushed.

Micah chuckled. "That's your cue, Dad." He glanced at Greg. "Smart move. It's always best to just nod and agree. Makes for a far easier life in the long run."

Greg gave him a half smile. "I'll bear that in mind."

"And after breakfast, before you take up residence on the couch, you can go into my office and call your mom," Dad added as he put the pan on the stove.

Greg blinked. "Oh. Okay. Thank you."

Dad beamed. "See? We're all gonna get along great. All you have to do is do exactly what I say."

Micah leaned closer to Greg and said in a stage whisper, "We let him think he's in charge. It makes him happy."

Greg snickered, and quickly reached for his glass of water. His pallor had lessened, for which Micah was thankful. The meds might make Greg woolly-headed, but that had to be better than the pain.

A CHRISTMAS PROMISE

And maybe the meds will make the call to his mom a little easier. It was obvious to Micah that Greg wasn't happy about the prospect, which only made Micah curious to know more. *What's the deal with his family?*

He had a feeling they'd know soon enough. One thing seemed certain: they had a lot to discuss over the coming days.

Greg stared at the phone in his lap. The office door was closed. Joshua had gone to the store, and Micah had said something about working on a canvas. Greg suspected they were giving him space and privacy, which he greatly appreciated. It was only when he started to tap out the numbers that he realized it was a harder task than he'd anticipated.

When was the last time I dialed from memory? It was all too easy to press a single key. *We're letting our brains go dull by relying on technology.* Greg knew he was procrastinating, but he couldn't help it. Anything to put off the moment. Sighing, he concentrated for a minute or two, until he was sure he had the right number. The phone barely had chance to ring twice before it was answered.

"Hello?" His mom sounded almost cautious, then Greg realized she didn't recognize the caller.

"Mom? Hi."

"Gregory Michael Chambers, where are you?" Her voice was so loud, he had to hold the phone away from his ear. "And why aren't you answering your phone? I've called, I've left messages on Facebook, I've sent texts...."

Greg's chest tightened, and his throat thickened. "Yeah, I'm sorry about that." The words came out as a croak. "I lost my phone." That was true, technically.

There was a pause. "Are you all right, sweetheart? You don't sound so good."

He cleared his throat. "I'm fine." Then he reconsidered. "Okay, not all that fine, if I'm honest."

She sighed. "You've had me so worried."

Greg almost dropped the phone in surprise. "Really?"

"Well, of course. What with your dad... dying, and you calling to say you weren't coming home right away... I figured you were just taking some time for yourself. But I haven't heard from you in two weeks. Of course I was worried. We both were."

He hadn't expected that. "I didn't think you'd have time to be worried. You have too much to do."

Mom chuckled. "Yes, well, taking care of two-year-old twin boys who both have colds... and then Damon comes down with man flu, so basically my life is hell right now. I'm also not sure about who exactly is the bigger baby—the twins or him."

Greg knew his mom and Damon hadn't planned on having kids: the twins had been a bit of a shock, especially as mom had just passed her fortieth birthday when she discovered she was pregnant.

"So where are you now?"

Her question dropped Greg back into the present. "I'm in Wyoming."

"Still? What on earth are you doing there?"

"I had a promise to keep, that I made to Dad." Silence fell. "Mom?"

"You're an adult. I can't tell you what to do anymore, I know that. You're twenty-four, almost twenty-five, and you have a mind of your own, but… there are things I never told you about your father." A pause. "I just don't want you to be shocked if you learn things about him that—"

"Are you talking about him being gay?" Greg blurted out.

The silence was almost deafening.

"Is that why you two split up? Is that what he meant about living a lie?" Now it made sense.

"He… told you he was gay?"

Greg sighed. *If only.* "No, mom, he didn't say a word."

"Then how did—"

"He asked me to deliver a letter. Well, I got to read it."

Another pause, and his mom's voice changed subtly. "He wrote to Joshua, didn't he?" All of a sudden, his mom sounded tired… resigned.

"You knew about Joshua?" Greg's world gave a little wobble. "When did he tell you?"

"We'd been married about six months. I was already pregnant. Except… if I'm honest, I knew there was someone, long before then. I just didn't expect it to be a guy."

"But… he married you. He must have loved you." Even as he said the words, he could see part of the letter dancing before his eyes. Something about his dad never loving her the way he'd loved Joshua.

"I suppose it's all right to tell you everything,

now that you can understand. We became good friends when he first came to my high school. We were both in our final year. There was something about him, an air of… sadness, I suppose. A mysterious quality. When we left high school, we stayed friends. His parents were very keen for us to marry." She chuckled. "You can say that again. I was married at nineteen." She sighed. "But I was fine with that. He was handsome, intelligent, and he could be really funny. Hell, at eighteen, all I could think of was marrying him and having his children."

"Then what happened?"

"We got married, of course. Instead of going to college, he got a job, and his parents bought us a house. I wanted to start having kids right away, but he wasn't so sure." She laughed bitterly. "I suppose the signs were always there. He was never that keen on… Never mind. I wore him down, and I was so happy when I found out I was expecting you."

"You said he told you when you'd been married for six months."

"Yes. That was when I realized my dream life was a lie." Another pause. "It was the last thing I expected to hear, that he was gay. That he'd been in love, and had lost him. That he didn't think he could cope with… living life as a straight man. I begged him not to leave. I told him I'd make him happy."

A wave of sorrow washed over him. "I'm guessing he stayed." They hadn't split up until Greg was three.

She huffed. "I knew he stayed because I was pregnant. And give him his due, he did try, really. It didn't help matters, of course, that I knew deep down he wasn't happy. And now that I think about it, that was the problem. That knowledge was always there, like a rift between us. Once you were born, I thought he'd settle down, get used to being a father. I didn't know how deeply the guilt was slicing into him."

"He couldn't stand living a lie."

"No, he couldn't." Her voice was soft. "He told me he was no good for me, that he was destroying my life as surely as he was destroying his own. He told me I deserved to be happy, with someone who loved me totally, in a way he never could."

"And what about me?" Greg could understand not wanting to stay in the marriage, but he'd left and had virtually severed all contact with them. Sure, there had been cards and presents for birthdays, Christmas, graduation… But no visits.

"Aw, sweetheart. Your dad did love you. I think he felt he'd already ruined my happiness, he didn't want to ruin yours too. Like he was bad luck or something. And then when Damon came along, your dad was so happy for me. He was glad you'd have a father figure in your life, someone you could rely on, depend on…. Not like him, he said."

Greg had been the one to make the first forays into forging a relationship with his dad. Greg had waited until he was twenty-one before contacting him. Now at least, he finally understood his dad's reticence. It had taken several phone calls and a lot of emails before he'd agreed to see Greg. "He really believed I'd do better without him, didn't he?"

"When you first told me you were going to see him, I was so worried. I thought it would end badly, that you'd come home a mess. But… you didn't."

"Maybe it was because he was older," Greg

reasoned. His dad had just celebrated his forty-first birthday, and Greg had gone to stay with him. What surprised him was how well they got on. Greg had travelled to Jackson, unsure of what to expect. What he'd found was a quiet, reflective man with similar tastes in books, movies and music. A man he'd really liked, enough that when he learned his dad was dying, it had almost shattered him.

"Are you okay, sweetheart?"

He knew what she was asking. "He's been gone a month, but yes, it still hurts." Now there was a new edge to his pain, an added dimension. Now Greg knew exactly what he'd lost.

"I know. And of course it still hurts. So sad you had so little time with him, but at least you got to know him. So where are you in Wyoming?"

He bit back a chuckle. "If I told you, I don't think you'd believe me. Let's just say I'm among friends." She didn't need to know about the previous week, not yet, anyway. And Greg wasn't sure he could cope with his mom's angst right then. "And speaking of my friends, this is their phone bill I'm charging up, so I'd better finish soon."

"Wait a moment. You said you'd read your dad's letter. How did you manage that?"

"I delivered it to Joshua… who let me read it." He wasn't about to tell her who he was staying with. He wasn't sure how that would be received.

"I see. Are you coming home for Thanksgiving?"

He sighed. "Actually? I was thinking about staying here. Would you mind?" He didn't want to hurt her, but he wasn't about to contemplate traveling to San

Diego in his present state. Besides, there were still questions to be answered.

"Of course I mind. Families should be together at Thanksgiving. But… I do understand. Promise you'll keep in touch? Can I call you on this number? Will you be there for a while?"

"I'll be here," he reassured her. "Try not to get too frazzled with the twins? And don't put up with Damon's man flu any longer than you have to. Tell him to man up."

She snorted. "Yeah, I can see *that* remark going down well." She paused. "I'm sorry I waited so long to have this talk. I should have said something a long time ago."

"No. It was always Dad's place to share that with me. You did the right thing." *Only Dad didn't, did he?*

Somewhere in the house, he heard Micah singing a Frank Sinatra song. Greg smiled. "Sorry, mom, I have to go. I'll call soon, okay?"

"Not if I call you first," she said. "Take care, Greg. Love you."

"Love you too." He disconnected the call, conscious of all the things he'd left unsaid.

They would have to wait.

Chapter Eight

"Is he okay? He seems really quiet this evening." Dad kept his voice low while he loaded the dishwasher.

Micah knew exactly what he meant. "It's not just this evening. He's been like this all day." Greg had seemed subdued, and though Micah had tried to raise a smile, his efforts had clearly fallen short.

Dad shrugged. "Maybe he has a lot on his mind." He leaned closer. "Do you think it has something to do with that phone call to his mom?"

It was the only suggestion that made any sense. "Let's find out." Micah poured out three mugs of coffee, and then picked up two of them. He walked into the living room, Dad following him. Greg was sitting on the couch, his leg propped up. The TV was on, but the sound was turned down. Not that Greg was watching it. He was staring at the fire.

Micah walked over to the couch and handed him one of the mugs. "Here you go."

Greg flashed him a tight smile. "Thanks."

Micah wasn't about to let that distract him from his course of action. He sat beside Greg, picked up the remote, and switched off the TV.

Greg blinked. "What was wrong with that show?"

Micah gave a casual shrug. "I don't know. I wasn't watching it. More to the point, neither were you. So I thought our time would be better spent trying to figure out what's eating you."

Greg frowned. "Nothing's eating me."

Dad snorted. "Son, I may not have known you all that long, but I know bullshit when I hear it."

Micah rolled his eyes. Sometimes, Dad could be about as subtle as a train-wreck.

Greg glanced at Micah, his lips twitching. "I don't recall your dad ever being this... blunt before."

Micah nodded. "Yeah, well, you've obviously never had a conversation with him when his bullshit detector was working properly. He's just had it repaired."

It took a second or two for his words to register, then Micah heaved an inward sigh of relief when Greg chuckled. "Bullshit detector. I like that."

"So does that mean you're gonna stop lying to us, and tell us what's wrong? You never know. Maybe we can help."

Greg sighed. "It's nothing that can be fixed, honest. I... I was thinking about stuff my mom told me. I guess it's just taking its time sinking in."

"What kind of stuff?" Dad leaned forward in his armchair.

"Well, for one thing..." Greg looked him in the eye. "Mom knew about you."

"Wait—what?" Micah sat upright. "You don't mean... your mom *knew* that your dad loved my dad?"

Greg nodded. "He told her, before I was even born. Hell, all *I* said was that I'd delivered a letter for Dad, and she came right out with your name, Joshua, just like that."

"I'm damn sure that's not what's got you thinking," Dad commented quietly.

"No, you're right about that. She was telling me about why my dad left, why he stayed away." Greg sipped his coffee. "I guess it was a conversation that needed to happen."

"The way you're talking, it doesn't sound like it was a bad conversation," Micah remarked.

Greg shrugged. "That's because it wasn't."

Micah scrubbed his hand over his cheek. "Then I don't get it. Why are you so... reluctant to go home? Why did you say in the hospital that you weren't sure you had a home anymore?"

"Oh, I see." Greg stared into his coffee for a moment. "Okay. When Mom met Damon, my stepdad, I was fine with it. He was obviously good for her."

"How old were you at the time?" Dad asked.

"Six or seven, I guess. Damon was the only father I'd ever known: I had no memories of my own dad. Anyhow, we got along fine. I liked him."

"Then what went wrong?" Micah asked softly.

"Nothing went wrong, as such. I went off to college, and they were both so proud of me. I didn't have to worry about student loans or anything like that. Mom and Damon paid partly for my studies, and the rest was paid for from a trust fund that Dad had set up when I was born." He expelled a breath. "So strange, now I think about it. He wouldn't stay, for fear of ruining our lives, yet he cared enough to make sure my schooling was taken care of."

Micah wasn't sure he fully understood some of that comment, but he let it go. "So you went to college. And?"

"I'd just received my Bachelors, and had gone home for summer vacation. When I got there, Mom had some surprising news for me. After fifteen years of marriage, she and Damon were going to have twins."

"Wow." Dad grinned. "I don't envy her, no, sir."

"Yeah, it was kind of a shock to both of them. But after that, everything changed."

"How?" Micah wanted to know.

Greg took a mouthful of coffee before responding. "Every time I went home for a weekend, or for the holidays or summer, it felt like… it wasn't my home anymore. Like I didn't belong there. Damon and Mom had the twins, and their whole life revolved around them. I just felt like I was in the way." He shook his head. "I'm not saying they shut me out, or anything. It's just that their focus changed." Greg frowned. "Don't get me wrong. I'm not saying I was jealous of my new little brothers, believe me."

"I don't think that for a second," Dad said promptly. "I think I understand what you mean. You grew up believing your dad didn't want you, which I suppose is common among kids whose parents divorce early. Then your mom has not one, but two children late in life. One minute you were the center of her universe, and the next? You felt… replaced. I can imagine that would only make you feel… alienated, somehow."

Judging from Greg's expression of astonishment, Micah guessed his dad had nailed it. "Then what happened?" He knew there was more to come.

"So I went back to school to do my MBA. I spent less time at home. When I was finished with my studies, that was about the same time I found out about Dad's diagnosis. I told Mom I was going to stay with him awhile." He swallowed. "I ended up staying five months, until the day he died."

"You… were with him?" Micah knew all too well what that felt like.

"Yes. I was there for the funeral too. He'd paid for everything ahead of time, and there wasn't anything for me to do, but stand there and mourn him. Hardly anyone was there, and that made me so sad. He'd moved to Wyoming to start a new life—he even went back to school— and yet, by the time I got to know him, he had no life to speak of."

Micah jerked his head up at that. "Wyoming?" He glanced at his dad, who seemed unperturbed by this. "Did you know where he lived?"

Dad shook his head. "I only found out when I read the letter."

He shoved down hard on his frustration, and kept his voice even. "Before either of you says another word, I think I need to read this letter for myself. Unless you object?"

Greg opened his eyes wide. "You haven't read it yet? I sort of assumed Joshua intended on showing it to you."

Dad got up from his chair. "I'm sorry, Micah. You're right. You need to read it too." He left the room.

Micah stretched out a hand toward Greg. "I know what you went through. With your dad, I mean. I was there when my mom…." His throat seized up.

To his surprise, Greg clasped his hand tightly. "I know, it hurts. I don't expect that will ever go away entirely." They sat there in silence, connected by their grief in a surprisingly intimate moment.

Dad coughed, and Micah pulled his hand free of Greg's. Dad held out the folded sheets. "Here."

Micah took them and sat back against the cushions. The only sound in the room was the crackling of the fire, the hisses that came from the logs. He read it slowly, trying to take it all in. Then he raised his head and stared at Dad, but the words wouldn't come. Tears pricked the corners of his eyes.

"I know," Dad said simply. "I think I've read it over twenty times since Greg gave it to me." He cleared his throat. "I don't know about you two, but I've had enough tears for one day. I think we should do something to lighten the mood."

Micah wiped his eyes. "Sounds good to me. What did you have in mind?" He could understand Dad not wanting to talk about it. And that letter… so much emotion in so few words.

Greg nodded. "I'm with you. It's been quite a day."

Dad went over to the bookshelves next to the fireplace. "I vote for a movie and popcorn, and I know exactly what I want to watch."

Micah caught Greg's gaze. "Be afraid. Be very afraid. Dad's taste in movies is almost as bad as his cooking." He winked, and Greg smothered a snicker. Relief flooded through him at the lightening of the mood in that room. *Nice one, Dad.*

"Just for that, you get to go make the popcorn. I'll have chocolate caramel, please. And make Greg whatever he wants. We got cheddar cheese, caramel, you name it." Dad beamed at him. "Well, get to it, popcorn boy."

Micah shook his head. "Uh uh. Not until you share which movie you're thinking of putting on."

Dad's smile morphed into something almost wistful. "Star Wars, Episode IV."

Micah could live with that.

Greg was feeling nervous.

Not that he had anything to feel nervous about. He was only going to meet Naomi, after all. Why meeting Micah's nineteen-year-old sister should bother him so much, he wasn't sure, but he'd had butterflies in his stomach all day.

Micah and Joshua hadn't helped matters. They'd started discussing the preparations for Thanksgiving, and Greg had asked if there was anything he could do to help, providing he could do it while seated. Joshua had glanced at Micah, before nodding.

"Now you mention it, there *is* an important task you can do."

"Sure, name it." Anything to stop feeling so useless.

Joshua's eyes gleamed. "You can be the turkey plucker this year. Can't he, Micah?"

Micah nodded solemnly. "I think so. That's a really important task."

"Turkey… plucker?"

Both of them nodded again. "Around here, we have to go out and catch the turkey first, but Micah and I will take care of that. Can't really ask you to do *that*, can we? Not when you're on crutches."

"You have to catch the turkey?" Greg knew Wright was in the middle of nowhere, but surely not….

"Uh huh." Micah smiled. "This is a big honor, you know. It takes years of training to be a fully-fledged turkey plucker." Then his lips twitched, and that glint in his eyes suddenly made sense.

"You pair of—"

"Careful now," Joshua admonished, grinning. "Insulting your hosts will result in significantly smaller portions tomorrow."

Greg arched his eyebrows. "I can't make up my mind whether that's meant to be a threat or a promise."

Micah guffawed. "You're quick. I like that."

Judging from Joshua's grin, he liked it too.

"They're here!" Micah called out.

Greg was yanked into the present, his butterflies going on a rampage in his belly. Joshua had gone to Gillette to meet Naomi's bus.

Micah came into the living room and gave him a stern glance. "You look fine, she's dying to meet you, and she doesn't make a habit of eating people." He grinned. "Well, she might nibble you a little."

"You are *not* helping. Again."

Micah opened his mouth, no doubt to say something witty, but was cut off when the door opened and a young woman with long, dark brown hair entered the room. She marched right over to the couch and stood beside it, staring down at Greg with ill-concealed interest.

"So you're Greg? You don't look like you got bashed." She looked him up and down. "I thought you had a cast on your leg."

Greg had to smile. "Amazing what a pair of sweats can hide, isn't it?" She was so like Joshua: they both had the same brown eyes, the same blunt way of expressing themselves.

Then she smiled, and her eyes lit up just like Micah's did. "Have these two been looking after you? Were you always this skinny, or is that how you've gotten after six days of avoiding my dad's cooking?"

Greg was more than ready to defend Joshua. "I like your dad's cooking. It's good."

Naomi stared at him, her mouth open. Then she swiveled to look at Micah. "You didn't tell me he'd suffered a head injury too. Poor boy's obviously delusional."

Joshua snorted. "'Poor boy', she says, like you're some little kid, when you're almost Micah's age."

"It's fine, Joshua." Greg grinned. "I can take care of myself."

Naomi studied him for a moment, her eyes shining. "Apparently." She turned to Joshua. "I suppose you haven't started preparing all the vegetables yet. I'm guessing you're gonna leave that to me and Micah again." She flicked her gaze back to Greg. "Having said that… *you* might make a pretty good kitchen assistant."

"Whatever I can to do be of help," Greg said with a smile. "But I'd recommend giving me tasks that don't require movement. I'm pretty lethal with those crutches."

"That's okay," she replied with a sweet smile. "I'm pre-med. I could always practice my bandaging techniques."

Greg snickered and met Micah's gaze. Micah gave him the thumbs up.

What on earth was I nervous about? Naomi was adorable.

Greg was suddenly looking forward to Thanksgiving.

Chapter Nine

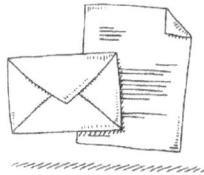

Greg awoke to the wonderful aroma of roasting turkey. He glanced at the clock beside the bed. Seven-thirty? *What time do these people get up in the morning?* Hell, it was still dark outside. He lifted his leg off the bed and pulled on his robe, before grabbing his crutches. The painful throb down his thigh that accompanied his first steps told him the first order of the day would be his meds. He shoved the capsules into the pocket of his robe and hobbled out of the room, heading for the kitchen, the enticing aroma tugging him along.

God, that smells good.

The kitchen was a hive of activity. Naomi was in the process of basting the turkey, with Joshua standing beside her, watching intently. Micah was seated at the table, a heap of sweet potatoes and carrots in front of him, which he was peeling. In the middle of the table stood a delicious-looking pumpkin pie.

"You baked already?" Greg was seriously impressed.

Naomi whirled around to give him a friendly smile. "Good morning! Well, it was when *I* got up. And don't be fooled by the pie. It was a store bought frozen one." She went back to her basting.

"Aw, don't tell him that, you'll shatter the illusion," Joshua moaned. "And watch what you're doing. You're dripping turkey juices onto the floor."

"Shit wipes off, Dad," Micah said, adding a peeled carrot to the pile.

"And you can watch your mouth." Joshua glared at him.

"I can cope with a little swearing," Greg told him. "And that's the first time Micah has cussed since I've been here, so I think he's doing okay." He flashed Micah a grin, which Micah returned, his eyes sparkling. Then his leg throbbed again, and the urge to smile left him.

Micah's eyes widened, and he pushed back his chair, lunging to his feet. "Hey. I think you need to sit down. Naomi, bring some cushions through, please?" He helped Greg onto a nearby chair. The throb morphed into a dull ache, and Greg didn't even try to refuse Micah's help. Micah filled a glass with water and handed it to him. "Got your meds?"

Greg nodded, and pulled them from his pocket. In the process, his robe loosened, revealing his torso.

Micah let out a hiss. "Shit, Greg. What the hell did they do to you?" Naomi approached, her arms full of cushions, and her mouth fell open. Joshua's brow furrowed, and he pressed his lips together.

Greg closed the robe, tying it more tightly. "Trust me, the bruises looked much worse last week." Now they were nothing but varying shades of yellow, but he knew the sheer number of them had to be a shock.

"I hope the police catch those bastards," Naomi muttered as she placed the cushions on another chair. Joshua glared at her, but she glared right back at him. "Oh, come on. Tell me you weren't thinking the same thing. Some people are just scum. I mean, who does that to a person? Beats the crap out of them, then leaves out in the middle of nowhere?"

Joshua sighed. "I apologize for my daughter, Greg. She used to be a sweet little thing before she went off to college." He aimed another glare in her direction. "Where apparently, she's learned some bad habits along with her studies."

"Nothing to apologize for," Greg said firmly. "But can we change the subject? This is killing the Thanksgiving vibes around here." Carefully he lifted his leg onto the chair, wincing.

"Take your meds," Micah said in a stern voice. "Now."

Greg arched his eyebrows. "Yes, *Dad*." He popped two capsules into his mouth and swallowed half the water. "That better?"

"Much. And you can sit there until they take

effect. It's still way too early for you to be on your feet a lot. Didn't the doc say it would be a couple of weeks before you'd be mobile?"

Part of Greg was touched by Micah's concern. He really was looking out for Greg, had been since Greg had arrived in their home. But at the same time, Greg hated the feeling of being useless. "Are you sure there's nothing I can do to help?"

"I *may* let you mash the potatoes later." Micah grinned. "But only if you're a good boy and do as you're told."

Greg lifted one of his crutches. "I can reach you with this, and I've got a good aim. Just saying."

Micah laughed. "Want some coffee?"

"That would be great. And that turkey smells amazing."

Naomi chuckled. "Wait till you try the stuffing. My mom's recipe. Now *that's* amazeballs." Her smile faltered, and Joshua rubbed her back.

"How about I make us some breakfast, now that we're all awake?" Micah stared at the kitchen table. "If we clear some of this out of the way first."

"Do we have any of that sausage gravy still in the freezer?" Naomi asked. "And biscuits? Or did you two eat them all?"

Greg's stomach rumbled. "Biscuits and gravy?" He hadn't had those for breakfast in a long time.

Joshua grinned. "I think we have a winner. I'll put the vegetables into water, and you two can make breakfast." He winked at Greg. "Seeing as my cooking is so awful."

"You can make the eggs. They're usually edible."

Micah dodged the towel that Joshua flicked toward his ass.

"Do you see what I have to put with?" Joshua said with a sigh.

Greg thought they were all wonderful.

"Where's Greg?" Naomi asked as she covered the cooked turkey with foil.

"In his room, asleep. I think those pills knock him out." Micah had helped Greg to his room, and before he'd even covered him with the comforter, Greg had fallen asleep.

Naomi checked the pans on the stove. The vegetables would be the last part of the meal to be cooked. The cranberry sauce was made, the sweet potatoes were ready to be roasted… They'd done really well.

"She'd be proud of us, you know," he said quietly.

Naomi turned to look at him and Micah noted the gleam of tears. "I was thinking the same thing."

Micah didn't hesitate. He pulled her into a tight hug, their cheeks pressed together. They didn't *do* this. Grief was a luxury to be denied when Dad was around, because they had to keep it together for his sake. They had to be strong for him, so tears were for when no one was around to see them. Right then Dad was safely ensconced in his office, and therefore out of sight.

"I miss her so much," Naomi whispered. "Especially now. God, the first thing I remembered this morning was how Mom used to wake us up with hot chocolate at Thanksgiving."

Micah snickered. "Only because she knew that was the fastest way to get us out of bed."

Naomi laughed quietly. "True." She held him against her, arms wrapped around him. "Do you think about her?"

"All the time." It didn't help that Christmas was almost upon them. "Maybe having Greg around will make things easier for Dad this year. You know, give him something to occupy him."

Naomi pulled away, her forehead creased into a frown. "Are you saying Greg will still be here at Christmas? Just how long is he staying with us? And while we're on the subject, wanna tell me why Dad invited a stranger to come stay with us? Was he just being a Good Samaritan?"

"Hey, I was going to ask him to stay, only Dad beat me to it."

"But why?" Naomi cocked her head to one side. "What is it you're not telling me?"

Before Micah could figure out how to respond, Dad walked into the kitchen. "Any coffee left?"

Naomi drummed her fingers on the countertop. "Tell you what. I'll make you some fresh coffee, if you give me some answers."

"Naomi, please, don't." Micah's stomach churned.

She whirled around and glared at him. "Don't what? Try to work out what's going on?" She turned to stare at Dad. "Well? Wanna tell me why you invited Greg to stay?"

"He's got a busted leg, and he needs time to heal."

"Uh uh." Naomi folded her arms across her chest. "Not buying it. You two are hiding something, and I want to know what it is—and *why* you think you need to hide it from me." She frowned. "I'm nineteen. I'm not a kid anymore."

"That's debatable," Micah muttered, and she glared at him. He couldn't tell her. That had to be Dad's decision.

"It's okay, son. Naomi's right. She's an adult now." Dad sighed. "I guess I thought there were some things about her dad that she didn't need to know just yet."

Naomi paled. "Dad? You're scaring me."

"Dad, just let her read the letter. It's for the best."

Dad nodded, and left the room. Naomi watched him go, standing so still, her arms by her sides. Micah put his arm around her shoulders. "It's all right, there's nothing to be scared of. Greg had a letter on him, addressed to Dad. It was from Greg's dad, who died a month ago, and it was his last wish that Greg deliver it."

Naomi stared at him. "This sounds serious. Not to mention intriguing. They knew each other? Since when?"

Dad re-entered the kitchen and handed her the envelope. "There are some photos in there, of me and Greg's dad, when we were seventeen. Before I met your mom."

She stared at the envelope. "I think I'm gonna

read this in my room, if you don't mind." Before they could say a word. Naomi walked out.

Dad swallowed. "What if—"

Micah rubbed his back. "You were afraid to let me know, and look how that turned out. What makes you think Naomi will be any different?"

"She's just a kid."

Micah opened his eyes wide. "How old was Mom, when you two first started dating?"

"Eighteen."

"And when you asked her to marry you?" Micah already knew the answer.

"Nineteen."

Micah smiled. "Nineteen's not so young, is it? And Naomi's had to grow up a lot since…." He knew how alike Naomi and Mom had been. She had Dad's way of expressing herself, but her temperament was Mom through and through.

To his surprise, Dad pulled him into a hug. "I know I don't say this enough, but you two… I couldn't have gotten through the last two years without you."

"This is what families do, right?" Micah's face brushed against Dad's scratchy chin. Then he broke free of the hug. "I'll make the coffee. And we can start dinner soon, once Greg wakes up."

"Let him sleep. It's good for him." Dad smiled. "You know what's weird? Greg seems to have slotted into our lives like he just… belongs there."

Micah knew what he meant. Just over twelve days since he'd found Greg, and yet it felt longer. Greg was easy to talk to and fun to be with. There was a lot they didn't know about him yet, but being with him felt… good.

"Wow." Naomi stood in the doorway, the letter and photos in her hand. She stared at Dad. "I... don't know what to say. Except... wow."

Dad frowned. "Good wow or bad wow?"

She shook her head. "Still trying to get my head around the fact that my dad is bi. Not that it's all that big a deal."

"It... isn't?"

Naomi widened her eyes. "Jeez, Dad, do you know how many of my friends are bi or gay? I mean, really? In my Biology class alone, we're talking gay, bi, trans, asexual..." She smiled. "Sometimes I feel like I'm in a minority." She held out the letter. "This is so sad." Naomi gazed at him inquiringly. "I gotta ask though. Did Mom know?"

"I asked the same question," Micah murmured.

"And I'll tell you both, only, not today, okay?" Dad sighed heavily. "I'm sorry, it's just that... the timing's not right. Let's just have the best Thanksgiving we can manage, all right?"

Micah knew his dad was having a hard time, what with the anniversary so close, but he was growing tired of the evasion. Not that he'd say a word. Micah could bide his time. "Sounds good to me."

"Dad?" Naomi smiled. "Let Greg stay as long as he wants, okay? I know it's weird, but it sorta feels like he's family."

Micah couldn't have been prouder of her than he was in that moment. "I second that."

Naomi flashed him a quick smile, her eyes gleaming. "Yeah, I thought you might."

"What does that mean?" Micah gave her a hard stare.

Naomi opened her eyes wide. "Nothing. Now, how about some coffee?" She chuckled and went to set up the coffee pot.

Micah groaned inwardly. Little sisters were a real pain in the ass, especially ones who read more into situations than was clearly there. He had an idea what she was implying, but he wasn't about to challenge it.

There were some arguments that were to be avoided, especially those he knew he'd lose.

Chapter Ten

Greg sighed contentedly. "I can't remember the last time I ate so much." He rubbed his very full belly. "I don't think I could eat another thing."

"Not even a wafer-thin mint with your coffee?" Micah asked with a sly grin.

Greg groaned. "Right now, there isn't even room for coffee. That and a mint might be the two last straws." He smiled to himself. He hadn't had Micah down as a Monty Python fan. It was good to know.

Naomi beamed. "Then we did a good job. Thank God for dishwashers, because the thought of all those pots and pans…" She shuddered.

"This is where we explain that Naomi has a phobia about rubber gloves," Joshua said in a loud whisper. "Almost to the point of being pathological." He snuck a glance in Naomi's direction, grinning.

Naomi scowled. "Now tell him the truth." When Joshua started laughing, she turned to Greg. "I was maybe five or six. My *dear brother* blew into a white rubber glove, tied it off, then stuck it on the end of a pole and lifted it up to my bedroom window. I saw this ghostly white, boneless hand floating outside, and became hysterical—at least, that was how Mom described it."

Greg couldn't help himself. He burst into laughter, picturing the scene in his head. "You're evil, aren't you?" he said to Micah. "How could you scare your little sister like that?"

"Duh. Because she was my little sister." Micah rolled his eyes. "Dad thought it was hilarious."

"Until Mom gave him a smack upside the head and told him he ought to be ashamed of himself," Naomi added. "The stories I could tell you about Micah…." When Micah glared at her, she gave Greg a sweet smile. "But I won't, because that would be mean of me, and I wouldn't do *anything* to jeopardize his chances."

"Chances?" Greg was at a loss.

"Well, seeing as you're just his type…" Naomi gave Micah a wicked grin. "He is, isn't he?"

Greg slowly turned to gaze at Micah, who had suddenly become very still. "Your… type?" Then it hit him. "You're gay?"

Naomi let out a gasp. "Oh my God. You didn't know."

"It's not like it's a secret, right?" Micah gave a shrug. "So I'm gay."

"You didn't say anything."

Micah frowned. "Why would I? It's not like I introduce myself to people by saying, 'Hi, I'm Micah, and I'm gay.' It doesn't define me, it's just... part of who I am."

"Given the conversations about our fathers' history these last few days, I think that would have been a good point to bring it up." He knew that wasn't what was bothering him. Greg was still hurting that he hadn't shared his own sexuality with his dad.

"I'm sorry. Naomi shouldn't have said anything. I don't mean the outing me part, I mean the implication that I'm... attracted to you. I don't want you to feel uncomfortable."

"Why would I feel uncomfortable?" Greg's heart hammered. "Either she's being a brat, and you're *not* attracted to me, or... it's true, and you..." He took a breath, forcing himself to keep calm.

"Look, I'm sorry too." Naomi flushed. "A lot of straight guys I know flirt with my gay and bi friends, and vice versa, but if you're not used to that, I can see how it might be awkward."

"Yeah, it might." Greg lifted his chin and looked Micah in the eye. "If I happened to be straight, that is. Which I'm not."

Silence fell around the table. Joshua looked from Greg to Micah, then back to Greg again. "Okay, something I need to ask here. Is there a gay gene that they've just discovered? Because the odds just seem astronomical. Hayden, you, me, Micah…."

"Not quite as astronomical as Micah being the one to find me on that particular road," Greg said softly. "And my dad never knew I was gay. I guess we ran out of time before I could tell him." His heart quaked.

Micah's brown eyes were warm. "I'm so sorry."

Greg swallowed. "This wasn't exactly how I imagined coming out would be." When three pairs of eyes focused on him, he gave a half-smile. "I never told anyone before, not even my mom." Only that wasn't quite true, and he knew it. Micah's family weren't the only ones who knew he was gay. Then he told himself that he hadn't once said he was gay that awful night. He hadn't needed to: his online profile statements had told those bastards all they needed to know.

"Can I ask… is this a recent thing?" When Greg arched his eyebrows, Joshua sighed. "Sorry, that didn't come out the way I intended. I meant to say, if you've only just come out, was it only recently that you thought you might be gay?" Joshua studied him closely. "Are you okay? Do you need a drink or something?"

Greg smiled at him. "I'm fine, thanks. And to answer your question, I guess it's fairly recent. One day I'll tell you about my epiphany, if I can call it that." He looked across at Micah. "Do you know how lucky you are? You have a wonderful family."

Naomi's face glowed, but she remained silent. Micah glanced around the table. "Yeah, I know."

Joshua cleared his throat. "Seeing as we all still have a drop of wine left, would you raise your glasses, please?" In silence, they did as instructed. "To family.

Those who are with us, those we've lost, and those who are new to us."

Greg's throat tightened. "To family." The words echoed around the room. He took a sip of wine. Micah smiled at him.

"Careful. That drop might just be the proverbial straw."

Greg laughed. "I'll take my chances."

This was shaping up to be the best Thanksgiving he'd ever experienced, and he knew that was due solely to the three people sitting with him.

It wasn't until Greg had lain awake for more than an hour that the reason for his insomnia came to him.

He'd forgotten to take his meds. Although it could equally have been that his stomach was still trying to digest the volume of food he'd guzzled. Then there was the conversation from after dinner. He hadn't anticipated *that* turn of events. Either way, he wasn't about to lie there in the dark, listening to the occasional gurgle from his gut. Maybe some warm milk would help. Not to mention a couple of capsules, because the ache in his thigh was just verging on becoming painful. Then he reconsidered. Pain meds plus wine were not a good combination. He'd have to put up with the pain.

Greg got out of bed, wincing as he took that first step with his crutches, before hurriedly lifting his leg off the ground. He inched his way to the kitchen, leaned against the countertop while he negotiated opening the fridge *and* holding a crutch, then removed the milk.

It wasn't until the milk was heating in the microwave, and Greg was staring out into the inky darkness, that he realized it wasn't totally black out there. A light was shining from somewhere close to the house, muted by a drawn shade. When the microwave stopped whirring, Greg swore he could hear music playing, very faintly. Piano music.

The milk forgotten, Greg made his way carefully to the back door at the end of the hallway. It wasn't locked, so he opened it as quietly as possible, peering through the gap to the rear of the house. The light came from a double garage, and the music was definitely coming from there too. Greg was relieved to find someone had cleared a path from the back door step to the side door of the garage, but ice glistened on the paving slabs. Carefully, so carefully, taking small steps, he went along the path and up to the door. He tried the handle, pushing down while holding onto one crutch. When it swung open, Greg felt warmth on his face, a welcome change after the cold night air.

"Greg? What are you doing out of bed?" The piano music came to an abrupt halt.

Greg stepped into the garage and caught his breath. "So this is your studio?" Everywhere he looked, there were paintings. They covered every available inch of wall space, and in some places they stood on the floor, leaning against each other, four or five canvases deep. Photos hung there too, images of landscapes taken in all seasons. The roof rose up to a point in the middle, and a ladder climbed up to a mezzanine floor that took up half the roof space. From where Greg stood, he could see yet more canvases. The only place not occupied by canvases was where a worn couch stood against the wall, but even then, paintings leaned against each arm, bracketing it. Near the large door stood a unit with a sink and a hot plate.

Micah sat behind an easel at the far end, partially obscured by a large canvas. He stared at Greg, a paintbrush still in his hand. "I was going to show you this place, once you were getting around more easily. Dad had a garage built at the other end of the house, so that I could use this one as a studio." He gazed at his surroundings. "This is every painting I've ever done."

"How old were you when you started painting?" From what Greg could see, Micah had a lot of talent. He'd hoped Micah wasn't one of those artists who slashed across a canvas with two or three bold stripes of paint, and declared it finished. Greg preferred paintings that were obviously *something*. Not that he would ever denigrate someone else's taste in art, but he knew what he liked, and he *loved* Micah's work.

Micah pointed to the upper floor. "Up there are paintings I did when I was eight or nine. Mom made me keep them." He gestured to the canvases piled around him. These are for my first art showing."

"Seriously?" Greg beamed. "That's great. When?"

"Next year. There's an art gallery in Gillette, the Frame Shop. They're giving me the space for a week. I'm making sure I have enough paintings. So far, the count is about fifty canvases."

Whatever reply Greg had intended to make was forgotten when his leg throbbed painfully. "I think I'd better… sit down." He stumbled over to the couch, lifting his leg onto the cushions. He sagged against them. "I might have overdone it."

Micah growled unhappily. "I knew I should have stopped you from having wine with dinner. You can't mix pills and alcohol. Is it hurting?"

Greg nodded. "But it's better now that I'm sitting." He peered at Micah. "Joshua told me you weren't a night owl. And I'm surprised to find you painting. He also mentioned something about you preferring natural light."

Micah chuckled. "Sounds like you and Dad have had quite a few conversations about me." He sighed. "He's right though. Usually, I'm not a night owl, but I couldn't sleep, for some reason. I thought if I came in here and worked for a while, it might help." He huffed. "Not that I've painted anything. And no, that wasn't because of the light. I've been sitting here, just… thinking, I guess." Micah stared at the canvas on the easel.

"What are you working on?" When Micah hesitated, Greg hastened to reassure him. "You don't have to tell me if you don't want to. For all I know, you don't usually let anyone see your paintings until they're finished."

Micah gazed at the canvas. "This isn't like the stuff I normally paint." Then he expelled a breath, picked up the canvas, and brought it across to where Greg sat. He turned it around, and Greg caught his breath.

"Is that… your mom?" He was gazing at a

portrait of a woman, with shoulder-length brown hair, deep brown eyes and a warm smile. The resemblance to Naomi and Micah was unmistakable. "It's beautiful." The rich copper sweater she wore accentuated her coloring.

"It's not finished." Micah stood it against a pile of canvases, then sat beside Greg on the couch, avoiding his leg. Micah perched on the edge of the seat cushion, his elbows on his knees, hands clasped between them, his gaze focused on the portrait. "I started painting it about five years ago. It was going to be a surprise for Dad's fortieth birthday. Only we never seemed to find enough time when he wasn't around. And then, when she got diagnosed with a brain tumor...."

"I'm so sorry." Greg's heart went out to him.

Micah stared at the portrait. "They operated and removed it. They said they got all of it. But she was never the same after that. She complained of double vision, amongst other things. She used to say there was a Gremlin inside her head, messing around in there. Then two years ago, in the week leading up to Christmas, she collapsed. We called for an ambulance, and they took her to Campbell County Memorial Hospital. She never recovered consciousness."

"Oh, God, Micah."

Micah twisted to face him. "She didn't die right away. The day after she arrived there, they were going to declare her dead, but when they turned off the machines, her heart kept right on beating. So the docs turned the machines back on. *Then* they said they couldn't declare her dead because there were still drugs in her system." He shook his head. "We saw the brain scans. We knew she couldn't come back from that. But no, they still wouldn't declare her dead. The third day—that was Christmas Eve—they finally made a decision and turned off the machines. We sat with her all day, watching that damn blip on the monitor, listening to her heart slowing down."

It was so close to what Greg had experienced with his dad, it was scary. "I know. I've been in that place too."

"Yeah?" Micah reached out and grasped Greg's hand, squeezing it. "It got to two in the morning. Dad and Naomi had stepped out to find some coffee, because we wanted to be awake when she…" His face tightened.

"I get it."

"Anyhow, at two-twenty-five, an alarm sounded, and God, it made me jump. It wasn't until later that I realized what it was." He smiled. "I reckon Mom set it off, to warn us to get our asses back to her bed before she went."

In spite of his heartache, Greg smiled. "I like that idea." Micah's fingers were laced with his, and it was a comforting feeling.

"By the time Dad and Naomi got back to her room, Mom had just gone. I held her hand while the line flattened out. Then I kissed her goodbye."

Micah's words finally registered. "So Christmas Day is—"

"Two years to the day that she died. Last year—Oh, God, Greg, last year was just awful. Thanksgiving was a mess, but we muddled through it. But then Dad wouldn't put up the lights. He refused to buy a tree. And when the day came, I wanted to just curl into a ball and cry myself to sleep. Only, I couldn't. Naomi and I talked about it, and we pasted on a brave face and shoved our tears way down deep where Dad couldn't see them."

"You were being there for him."

Micah nodded. "And we got him through it. Of course, we didn't celebrate. Mom would've been so angry with him. She was a Christmas nut. Every year, as soon as Thanksgiving had come and gone, out came all the holiday movies, and believe me, she had about a ton of them." He tilted his head to one side. "Maybe this year will be different."

"How so?"

Micah gave him a shy smile. "I'm hoping you'll still be staying with us, for one thing."

Greg stilled. "Really?"

"Sure. Unless you really wanna go traipsing across the country back to California. You're more than welcome to spend the holidays with us. It may even do Dad some good, to have another face around the place. You never know, he might even agree to us putting up a tree." Micah's smile grew sad. "She'd like that." He peered at Greg. "So? Will you stay?"

He needed to think about this. It couldn't be a spur of the moment decision. This required reflection and—

"Yes, I'd love to." The instant the words left Greg's lips, he was so happy he'd said them. Micah's face lit up.

"Great. I'll tell Dad in the morning."

Greg smiled. "It *is* the morning."

Micah let go of his hand and stood up. "Then maybe it's time we were both in bed." He bit his lip. "I mean, our own beds."

Greg snickered. "It's okay, I got that part." Come to think of it, he was suddenly bone tired. "Maybe you're right."

Micah held out his arms. "Then allow me to help you back to your room."

The way Greg's leg was aching, he needed all the help he could get. "Done."

By the time Micah had gotten him to his room, Greg's body was crying out for sleep. Micah surprised him by helping him out of his robe and into bed, pulling the comforter over him with care.

"Try to sleep. I'll see you in a few hours." Then Greg's heartbeat raced as Micah bent over and gently kissed his cheek. "Good night." The door closed softly behind him.

Greg lay there, his mind going over Micah's story. If he'd thought the family was wonderful before, that was as nothing compared to his opinion of them now. They'd gone through so much, and yet they'd emerged strong, connected… together. He closed his eyes, and Micah's image was right there, those deep brown eyes so like his mom's, the short, brown hair, the sweet smile.

Don't forget sexy. Because it surely was a very sexy smile.

The warm, sexy smile of a gay man who'd just kissed him good night. Now *that* was something to dream about.

Chapter Eleven

"Come on, Greg. Three more. Just three more."

Greg glared at Fran. "You want three more? Fine. *You* do them."

She sighed. "Okay, I know you're aching, and you've probably had enough, but you've been doing so well today."

It didn't feel that way to Greg. As far as he was concerned, the whole of their physical therapy session had been one complete ball ache from beginning to end.

They'd only started working together the previous week, so he knew it was early days, but he hadn't anticipated how much it was going to hurt.

"Sorry to interrupt your torture—I mean, exercises—but I'm making hot chocolate. Would you like some, Fran?"

She glanced over at Joshua and beamed. "I'd love some, Mr. Trant, thank you." She peered at Greg. "You can have some as a reward for doing the last three."

"Fine." He glared at her again. "Only I think he got it right the first time with 'torture'."

Fran grinned. She waited until Joshua had gone into the kitchen, then leaned closer. "You have *no* idea. So let's get these finished, then you can grab a shower before your cute friend finishes working out there. Wouldn't want to be all hot and sweaty when he walks in here, would ya?" Greg gaped at her, and she laughed. "These eyes don't miss much."

Greg narrowed his gaze. "*You* are evil."

Fran buffed her fingernails on her shirt. "Thanks. It sorta comes with the job." She put her hands on her hips. "I'm still waiting."

Grumbling to himself, Greg slowly lifted his left leg off the ground to a height of a couple of inches, held it there for a moment, then slowly lowered it again. Sweat popped out on his brow, but he repeated the motion two more times, before dropping his arm across his eyes. "No more."

Fran patted his arm. "No more. You did good." She helped him to sit on the couch, and then rolled up the mat on which he'd been exercising. "Okay. We'll carry on next week. In the meantime, *try* to do a little exercise every day? Just don't overdo it. You're still not ready to put your full weight on that leg yet, so don't even think about."

"Are you always this bossy?"

She grinned. "Always, so suck it up." Joshua walked into the living room to hand her a mug, and she sighed contentedly. "This is my reward too." Fran peered at Greg. "So what are you doing with the rest of your day?"

"Gee, I thought I might go for a run around the yard," he retorted. Joshua rolled his eyes as he handed Greg his mug.

"Sassy. I like that." Fran beamed. "Whereas *I* am going to the Home Depot to pick up a Christmas tree." She was almost buzzing. "Even if my dumbass boyfriend thinks it's too damn early. I told him this morning, today is December first, so I'm officially allowed to put up a tree. Hell, it's not like we haven't had the Festival of Lights since mid-November. I'm just catching up."

"Festival of Lights? What's that?"

Fran gaped. "How can you not know about that?"

Joshua coughed. "Maybe because he was in the hospital November tenth to the eighteenth, and since then he hasn't left this house. He hasn't had the opportunity to go to Gillette." He turned to Greg. "Gillette has had a festival of Lights for the past eleven years. There's a park over on Doubletree Lane that puts together displays, stuff like the Twelve Days of Christmas, Santa's Workshop, Penguins on Ice, a Nativity scene, and a whole lot more."

"They use over one million lights," Fran added, "and some of the displays are over fifty feet tall." She stared at Greg. "You gotta see it. Maybe Mr. Trant will take you."

"Thank you for that suggestion. I'll consider it." Joshua regarded her with arched eyebrows.

Greg wasn't all that surprised by Joshua's response, not after what Micah had told him. Christmas wasn't ever going to be the same for his family, understandably.

Fran waited until Joshua had left the room, before speaking in a low voice. "Maybe there's someone else who might wanna take you to see the lights." Her eyes sparkled.

Greg shook his head, chuckling. "You don't give up, do you?" Not that the idea didn't appeal to him. Micah, a million Christmas lights twinkling against a black sky, snow... He sighed inwardly. Just because he wanted it to happen didn't mean it was going to. In the week since Thanksgiving, Greg had slowly become aware of something.

He was crushing on Micah.

It had started with little things, like the way Micah smiled. One look at that smile, and warmth spread through Greg, a languid heat that crawled through every part of him. And then there were the little touches that seemed more prevalent; a hand on Greg's back: the way Micah would touch him on the arm or the hand while they were talking: and the way Micah would rub his shoulders when he knew Greg's leg was aching.

Of course, they might mean nothing. For all Greg knew, this was how Micah *was*, and Greg was simply becoming used to his manner. But that didn't stop him hoping. Greg asked himself countless times if his burgeoning attraction to Micah was because he knew Micah was gay, or if he'd have been attracted to Micah while knowing nothing of his sexuality. The conclusion he arrived at was always the same—it was Micah, pure and simple.

Not that Greg was going to act on his crush. Once his leg was healed, that would be him out of Wyoming and back to California, or wherever he ended up. Right then he was a guest in Micah's home, and Greg wouldn't do anything to jeopardize that situation.

"Greg?"

He gave a start. "Sorry. Guess I zoned for a second there."

"A second?" Fran snickered. "I've finished my hot chocolate and I'm ready to leave. You were off in your own little world." She waggled her eyebrows. "Hope you were sharing it with someone hot."

"Goodbye, Fran." Greg smiled. "See you next week. And I hope you find the perfect tree."

Fran laughed. "Well, I guess that's me given *my* marching orders." She ruffled his hair. "So long. Don't tire that leg." She walked out of the living room, and Greg heard muffled conversation. Joshua entered the room.

"How did it go? Is it getting any easier?"

Greg sighed. "Not so much that I've noticed."

In Joshua's hand was a glass of water and his capsules. "I thought you might need these."

"You're a lifesaver." His leg was just starting to ache again. He took one capsule, chasing it with water. "Is Micah still in his studio?"

Joshua nodded. "He's been working on that snowscape for a week now. He says it's almost finished."

It seemed like the perfect opportunity. "Have you got a minute?"

"Why, what's up?" Joshua sat beside him on the couch. "Is everything all right?"

"Do you think you could talk about my dad?" It was three weeks to the day since Micah had found him, and Joshua still hadn't done as he'd promised. Greg didn't want to pry—he just wanted to know a little more about his dad when he was younger.

Joshua regarded him in silence for a moment. "I *was* going to go into my office and work for a while."

Greg waved a hand, although his heart sank. "That's okay. I know you have work to do." Joshua was a software designer, and worked from home.

Joshua nodded slowly. "But I guess it's time we talked." He leaned back against the seat cushions. "What do you wanna know?"

Greg smiled. "Whatever you want to tell me. I only got to know him these last couple of years, and there's so much I don't know. Could you tell me how you met? What he was like?"

A slow smile spread across Joshua's face. "I could do that." He clasped his hands in his lap. "He used to hide my toy cars, you know."

"Really?"

Joshua laughed. "Yeah, the little shit. We'd be playing in my room, and I'd go to the bathroom, only to return and find he'd hidden all my cars. Then he'd start counting, seeing how long it would take me to find them all."

"How old were you two then?"

"Seven or eight, I think. We used to play hide and go seek in the Talladega Forest, and we'd ride our bikes along the trails too. There was always an element of danger too. We knew there were coyotes and black bears in the forest."

Greg stared. "Did you ever see them?"

Joshua nodded. "We built ourselves a hideout. It was only an old sheet that we covered with branches and leaves, then we'd crawl under it, and wait. Some days we'd lie there for hours, and all we'd see were squirrels, rabbits, raccoons, even turkeys. Once, we even saw a white-tailed deer." His face lit up. "God, it was such a beautiful, graceful creature. And then finally, we saw a bear. Lord, it was big. I don't think either of us dared breathe as it lumbered within a few feet of us."

"Sounds like you used to have fun." Greg hadn't had close friends when he was growing up. He'd been more of a loner. Come to think of it, things hadn't changed much while he was at college either.

"We sure did."

Greg sat spellbound as Joshua told story after story of their exploits. He got the impression that his dad had been a loyal friend, there for Joshua when he needed him. After he'd listened for a while, Greg got up the courage to ask something a little more personal.

"When did you know you loved him?"

Joshua stilled, then relaxed against the cushions once more. "I think I was fifteen when I first realized I was attracted to him. There had been a couple of girls in high school who I'd been interested in, but Hayden? There was something about him that... *pulled* me, I suppose, is a good way of putting it. I loved spending time with him. We'd talk for hours, about anything that entered our heads. Anyhow, there was a school dance before summer vacation. We'd just finished eleventh grade. I'd taken Betty Edwards, but Hayden had gone alone. Turned out, Betty was more interested in getting off with Declan Ridault than dancing with me." He chuckled. "Not that I really minded. I spent most of the evening sitting with Hayden, drinking soda and talking as usual. Except that night? You know what I really wanted to do, only I didn't dare?"

Greg smiled. "Dance with him?"

Joshua nodded. "Only, two guys dancing? In Alabama? Hell, no. I wasn't dumb enough to even suggest it. Anyway, at eight o'clock when the dance was over, a whole bunch of us went over to Pete's Smokehouse. It was a diner that played decent music. We had a great time, only I ate too much. Their BBQ pulled pork was to die for." He sighed. "When the joint closed at nine-thirty, we all left. Most people got their parents to collect them, but Hayden suggested we walk home. It was only a couple of miles." He smiled. "I wasn't gonna say no to that. A stroll in the moonlight? *That* was romantic."

"What happened?"

"We set off walking along 231, until we reached Imerys-Gantt's quarry, where there was an observation point. We'd been there on a field trip from school, to look at the marble. Hayden and I walked along the path that ran around the little man-made lake. He'd brought along a pocket flashlight, so I began thinking he'd planned this." Joshua had a faraway look in his eyes. "It was a beautiful night. The moon was full, and it was shining on the surface of the still water. I think I knew then what was coming."

Greg had a feeling he knew too.

"My heart was pounding so hard, I was sure he'd

hear it. I kept wondering what he was gonna say, because he just…stared at me, like he'd never seen me before. And then… he kissed me." Joshua's face took on such an expression of wonder that Greg's chest tightened. "It wasn't what I expected. He was so… gentle. Not how I thought a guy would kiss, ya know?"

Greg swallowed. "No, I don't, as a matter of fact." He gave a half smile. "Never been kissed, at least, not by a guy."

Joshua's eyes widened. Then he nodded sagely. "Your time will come. Just make sure it's with someone you really care for. Kisses like that are too precious to waste on just anyone." He chuckled. "Me and your dad sure shared a lot of kisses. That whole summer, I swear we were kissing every chance we got. Of course, the moment arrived when we knew we wanted… more." The skin around Joshua's mouth tightened, and Greg stiffened.

"What happened?"

"We had it all worked out. I was going to his place so we could study for a test. His parents were gonna visit some friends. We'd talked about nothing else for a couple of weeks. I was so nervous, my palms got clammy just *thinking* about it. Neither of us had… you know. And as it turned out, we didn't get the chance. His parents came home early."

"I think I know the rest."

"Yep, you do." Joshua sighed heavily. "I'm sorry things worked out the way they did. That letter… to know he'd been so close. God, to have just seen him one more time…." Then Greg's breathing hitched when Joshua shifted across the couch and hugged him. "Thank you," he murmured against Greg's hair. "At least I finally know that he never forgot me, just like I never forgot him."

Greg breathed in Joshua's warm, comforting scent. "I'm glad I decided to deliver it in person. I feel like I've gotten to know him a little better."

How long they sat like that, Greg had no idea. They pulled apart when Micah cleared his throat from the doorway. "Am I... interrupting?"

Joshua smiled. "No, I think we're about done." He peered at Greg. "Wouldn't you say?"

He nodded. "We're done." Then he turned to Micah. "You're just in time to make lunch." He grinned.

Micah snorted. "*How* long before you can get around without those crutches?"

"Not until after Christmas," Joshua interjected. "So you'd best do as Greg says and make lunch." He winked at Greg. "Besides, all *you've* been doing is painting."

Micah's jaw dropped. "All I've been—"

Joshua guffawed. "You should see your face. Sit down. *I'll* make lunch. You just rest your... paintbrush." And with that, he got up from the couch and walked out of the living room.

Greg couldn't help laughing, and it wasn't long before Micah was joining in. As he composed himself, it occurred to Greg that he cared a great deal for both men, but for very different reasons.

Chapter Twelve

"Naomi just emailed. She'll be home this weekend for the holidays," Dad said as he came into the living room where Micah and Greg were sitting on the couch, both reading.

Greg glanced up and smiled. "Great!"

Micah groaned. "Great. At least three weeks of aggravation." Not that he meant a word of it. The verbal sparring between them had gotten more interesting since she'd begun college. And the thought of getting through Christmas without her was inconceivable.

Dad chuckled. "You love her and you know it." He left the room.

Micah put down his book on photorealism. "Quick, while he's not here... I've had an idea."

Greg lowered his copy of Death In The Clouds and raised his eyebrows. "Did it hurt?" His lips twitched.

Micah rolled his eyes. "I swear, you've been taking lessons from Naomi behind my back. That girl could write a textbook on the subject: *How to annoy Micah*."

Greg grinned. "Glad to know all my studying is paying off. What's up?"

"I've been thinking. Maybe it's time to bring a little Christmas back into this house. I'm not talking how it used to be. Hell, Mom put enough lights on this house for it to be seen from outer space. No, I'm thinking about a tree. It would be a start."

"And you want my help."

Micah had to admit, Greg was fast on the uptake. "Exactly. All you have to do is follow my lead, and then show some enthusiasm for the idea."

Greg nodded slowly. "I can do that."

"You bastard!"

Micah jumped up. "Dad? What's wrong?" He ran to Dad's office, to find him shaking a fist at his computer monitor. "Er, Dad?"

"Stupid thing just died on me!" Dad glared at it. "So now I have to go buy a new one."

"Don't you have an old monitor that you can use? Or maybe you can—"

"I know you're trying to help," Dad interjected, "but it'll be a hell of a lot quicker in the long run if I just get in the truck and drive to Gillette." He gave the monitor another glare. When the phone rang, it got a glare too. "Now what?"

Micah left him to it. He returned to the living room, where Greg looked up at him questioningly. "Hardware issues," Micah explained. He sat down and picked up his book.

A couple of minutes later, Dad came back into the room and walked up to the couch.

"Greg, that was one of the detectives who interviewed you. He was calling to see how you were, and to ask if there was anything else you'd recalled about the… incident. I told him you'd call back if there was anything."

Greg closed the book and placed it on the arm of the couch. "I told them everything." His face took on that closed-off expression that Micah already knew so well.

"Sounds to me like they're no closer to catching anyone," Micah said quietly. "Not if they're asking that."

"I'd have to agree." Dad sounded almost subdued. "Anyhow, I'd better go to Gillette. I'll see you in a couple of hours." He left the room again, sighing.

Micah got up from the couch and wandered over to the window. He watched as Dad pulled the truck out of the driveway. "He really cares about you, ya know." Micah could see why: there was something about Greg that got under your skin.

Under my skin, into my head and then into my heart. Micah wasn't an idiot. He was well acquainted with that wonderful, glorious feeling of falling for someone. Of course, he'd never gotten past that to the stage where a particular someone took up permanent residence in said heart, but he lived in hope.

Then it struck him that Greg had gone very quiet. He turned to face the couch, and his gut clenched.

Greg had picked up his book once more. He was staring across the room at the fireplace, but Micah doubted he saw it. There was a distant look in his eyes, and his knuckles were white where he gripped the book tightly.

"Greg, what's wrong?" Micah sat beside him on the couch.

Greg blinked, and met his gaze. "I lied to the police." His voice cracked.

"What do you mean?" Cold spread through Micah.

"Well, I suppose it was more omission than lying, but the result is the same. I didn't tell them everything."

"But why on earth not?" Micah sprang to his feet. "Don't you want the police to catch whoever did this? Greg... you. Nearly. Fucking. Died." He raked his fingers across his scalp. "They left you in the middle of nowhere. If I hadn't come along when I did, you—"

"I *know*! Don't you think I know that?" Greg's eyes were anguished. "I couldn't tell them."

"Why? Give me *one reason why* that makes sense." Micah crouched beside him. "Please, Greg. I don't understand." He pried the book gently from Greg's hands and then took one of them in his. "Tell me what happened?"

Greg's breathing grew erratic, and all the color drained from his face. "I don't even want to *think* about that night, let alone describe it. Ever since I came around in that hospital, I've tried to forget it, only... it won't go away. Those pills may knock me out, but I don't think

I've slept a whole night through since I got here. That night keeps on playing over and over in my dreams. What makes it worse is that now and again, I'm scared that…" He shuddered out a breath. "What if… I wasn't the only one they did this to?"

"Who? What were they like?" Micah squeezed his hand. "Please, Greg."

"There… there were two of them."

Micah nodded, his gaze locked on Greg's face.

"I'd h-hitched a ride as far as Gillette," Greg stammered out. "The truck driver dropped me at a place called Jake's Tavern."

"I know it. On Douglas Highway." Micah stilled. "You were hitching?"

Greg nodded. "My plan was to find somewhere warm for the night, maybe a motel or a cheap hotel, and then continue on to Wright the next day. Only, I'd just spent four hours in a truck, and I wanted a drink. So… I went to the bar." He drew in a couple of deep breaths.

Micah tightened his grip on Greg's hand. "It's okay. Just let it out, all right?"

Greg took a gulp of air. "All right. So I was sitting at the bar, I'd had a couple of beers and I was feeling nicely… muzzy. A guy came up to me. Really cute guy, the kind you see photos of, and think, 'Why do I never see guys like that in real life?' You know? Anyway, this guy held up his phone, and there was my photo… my profile photo on Grindr."

It was Micah's turn to blink. "You're on *Grindr*? Hell, *I'm* not even on that." He wasn't interested in hookups and one-night stands, not that it would matter much if he was. Pickings were slim in Wright, and he wasn't about to venture further afield.

Greg huffed. "I just thought this was what gay men did. I got as far as uploading my details, then... I got cold feet. I never looked at it once. I was going to delete it, I just hadn't gotten around to it yet."

"So... he'd found you on Grindr."

Greg nodded. "He bought me a couple of drinks and we talked for a while, not about anything consequential, just innocuous stuff like movies and music. He steered clear of politics, which was fine by me. It's not one of my favorite topics of conversation."

"Did *he* give you a name?"

Greg nodded. "Jake. Not that I think he told me the truth. He asked me what I was doing there, and I told him. Then he said if I wanted a bed for the night, I could stay at his place. He lived in Gillette, and I could choose from the sofa bed or... his." Greg swallowed. "You know what they say—it seemed like a good idea at the time. It didn't occur to me until I was lying in the hospital, that for someone who had Grindr on his phone, who was inviting me back to his place to spend the night... he made no attempt to kiss me. Or even to touch me."

"What happened?" Micah asked softly.

Greg stared at their joined hands. "We got as far as his car. He was parked in the farthest corner of the parking lot. Only, when we got there, there was another guy already sitting on the passenger's side. That was when I got scared. I said something about changing my mind, but then the other guy hit me on the back of the head, and I went out like a light." He shuddered.

That was enough for Micah. He got up from his crouching position, and sat beside Greg, putting his arm around Greg's shoulders. "I gotcha." Greg shivered against him, and Micah pulled him closer.

"When I came to, I was freaking terrified. I was in the trunk of a car, my hands were tied behind my back, my ankles were tied together, and there was something stuffed in my mouth. Then… the car came to a stop, and I thought my heart was going to stop too. They opened the trunk, yanked me from it, and carried me between them. I had no idea where I was. All I could see was snow. There was a faint hum of traffic in the distance, and not a single light to be seen anywhere, only the flashlight they kept shining in my eyes."

"Why were they doing this? Did they give you any reason? Because it seems like a lot of thought went into this, just to rob someone."

Greg shook his head. "They weren't out to rob me. And I don't believe for *one single second* that either of them was gay. In fact, I think they used Grindr to… target me."

Micah froze. "Fuck, no."

"Micah, every time they landed a punch, every time they got in a kick, it was punctuated with some of the most homophobic slurs I've ever heard. I was under no illusion why they were beating the crap out of me—it was because I was gay. Not that I ever told them that. I didn't have to—they had all the proof they needed right there on his phone. And I'm pretty sure they only took my backpack, wallet and phone to make it look like it was a robbery." Greg covered Micah's hand with his own. "When you drove me here from the hospital, and you pointed out the spot where you found me… that was when it hit me. They'd dumped me there, in the hope that no one would find me." He swallowed hard. "They intended for me to die there. And I would have done, if not for you."

Micah couldn't help his response. He kissed Greg's temple. "But you made it. You *didn't* die."

Greg met his gaze. "When I came to briefly, I knew it wasn't where they'd beaten me up. I also knew I was near a road, because now and again I heard a car go by. Not that anyone could spot me where I was, so I... crawled through the snow, trying to get closer to the road. I made it, then passed out again." He shuddered. "Micah, what if that detective called because there's another case similar to mine? What if they're hoping I can give them anything to shed light on it?" He stilled. "What if... those two men have only just gotten started?"

Micah wanted to throw up. "Then you have to tell the police everything."

"I told them I got jumped on as I was walking along the highway. I didn't mention Jake's Tavern, Grindr, what... what they said to me... because I was just so... ashamed. Plus, I had no idea what the detectives' reaction would be. You hear such horror stories, Micah. There's still so much hate out there, and lately there seems to be more of it."

Micah cupped his chin. "If you want, I will go with you to the police. Dad, too. We will sit beside you while you tell them what really happened, and if we get so much as a sneer out of *anyone*, or even the vaguest hint of one, then we take it higher."

"Really?" Greg's eyes glistened, but he blinked away the tears that threatened to fall.

Micah nodded. "You are *not* on your own, okay? You have us in your corner now, and good luck trying to get rid of us, because we Trants can be pretty tenacious." He let go of Greg's face.

Greg gave a weak smile. "Aren't I the lucky

one?" His breathing evened out, and a little color returned to his face.

"It feels better, now you've told someone, doesn't it?" Not that Micah needed to hear Greg's reply—he could almost watch the tension seep from Greg's body. His breathing was slower, and he'd eased his grip on Micah's hand.

Greg nodded. "I'm not going to tell my mom what happened. I'll just make out that it was a vicious robbery. She's going to have enough to deal with, when I tell her I'm gay. I'm not expecting fireworks, by the way—she's not the sort—but yes, it will definitely be a surprise."

Micah snickered. "Remind me to tell you one day how I came out to my dad." He gazed into Greg's eyes. "Thank you for telling me," he said quietly.

Greg smiled. "It must be a Trant family trait. You're all so easy to talk to. You inspire trust."

"Good to know." All Micah wanted to do was lean forward and kiss Greg on the mouth, but he held back. *Not now, when his emotions are all over the place.*

There would be another time, and when it occurred, Micah would not be holding back.

Chapter Thirteen

Only one day to go until Naomi was home, and Greg was still waiting for Micah to take the lead in whatever he had planned to bring Christmas back into their home. Lights had already begun to appear along Willow Creek Drive, as more and more houses dusted off their decorations, getting ready for the holidays. Greg figured Micah was just waiting for the right moment, and obviously it hadn't made an appearance yet.

He put down his paperback and closed his eyes, content to sit on the couch and enjoy the fire's warmth.

Apart from their trip into Gillette that morning so that Greg could speak with the detectives, Greg's days were beginning to blur into one giant heap of non-activity, and he was doing his best to ignore the restlessness that poked and prodded him now and again. He knew the healing would be a slow process, but still....

Micah and Joshua had been amazing that morning. True to his word, Micah had sat beside Greg while he told Detective Riley everything, and Greg had gotten the impression that what Micah *really* wanted to do was hold his hand the entire time. Thankfully, Detective Riley had reacted positively, although his words had painted a more negative picture. Even if they ever caught the guys, the chances of them being charged with a hate crime in Wyoming were non-existent, at least for the present.

The phone's shrill ring shattered both the silence and Greg's recollections. Joshua came into the room, glancing apologetically at him. "Sorry, I forgot I'd left it in here." He answered the call. "Joshua Trant speaking." Joshua stilled. "Yes, he's right here. One moment, please." He held the handset against his chest. "It's your mom."

Greg blinked. It had been a couple of weeks since he'd called her. He held out his hand for the phone, and then Joshua left the room.

"Hi, Mom."

For a moment he thought they'd been cut off, but finally she broke the silence. "Joshua Trant? You're staying with Joshua Trant? And you didn't think that was worth mentioning? You said you were staying with friends."

He sighed. "Joshua and his family *are* friends.

They asked me to come stay with them, and I said yes." It was probably the best segue he was going to get. "In fact, I have a lot to thank them for."

"But… you've only just met them." He could hear the bewilderment in her voice.

"Okay, I'd better tell you the truth." Well, not all of it—as much as he felt he could share, and she could handle. "I… was robbed a few weeks ago. Pretty viciously, as it turns out. My attackers left me by the side of the road in the snow, and I ended up in hospital with a fractured femur, plus other bumps and bruises."

He couldn't miss her gasp. "Why didn't you tell me when we spoke?"

"Because you didn't need to know! You'd only have worried about me." Greg was starting to regret saying anything.

"What—like I'm worrying *now*, you mean? Come home, Greg. Let me take care of you."

He pushed out an exasperated sigh. "Mom, don't you think your life is full enough right now? How about you let me finish? Because I'm not done yet."

She huffed. "Fine. Finish."

"The guy who found me and brought me to the hospital? That was Joshua's son, Micah. He saved my life, Mom."

Another bout of silence. "Wow. Seriously?"

"I know, I know. I was amazed when I found out. And then Joshua came right away, and they stayed with me through the night. They visited me every day, and then they brought me here. I'm safe, I'm comfortable, and…." He took a deep breath. "They've asked me to stay for the holidays, and… I said yes."

"Oh. Oh, I see."

Greg closed his eyes. *Was I wrong to say yes? Is it so bad of me to want to spend time with Micah and his family?* When Micah had asked him, the night of Thanksgiving, Greg had simply been happy to be there. Since that night, however, things had changed. Another element had been added to the mix—his growing attraction to Micah—and the idea of spending the holidays with him filled Greg with excitement and anticipation.

"Mom," he said softly. "I've finished college. The next logical step is for me to find a job and a place to live. You knew I had to leave the nest at some point, right? And it's not as if the nest is empty. You're going to have a couple of chicks in there for at least another fifteen years."

She groaned. "Why did you have to go and say that? I've only just survived the terrible twos. Did you have to be so goddamn specific?" Mom sighed. "Sorry. I guess I'm feeling my age today."

"What is it they say? You're only as old as the man you feel, and seeing as Damon's younger than you, let *him* run around after the twins." Greg chuckled. "Marrying a younger man has to have *some* benefits, right?"

Mom laughed. "Now that you mention it...." Another sigh. "You're right, of course. I guess it hadn't sunk in properly that you've... left home."

"Wait until I find a place, and I turn up with a U-Haul to pick up all my stuff. *Then* it'll sink in."

"Yeah, before I know it, you'll be turning up on my doorstep with some girl, telling me you're gonna get married." She chuckled. "I'm gonna say this now, okay? I can wait a few years to become a grandmother. I have enough on my plate being a mom again. Don't feel you need to start having kids on my account, all right?"

Greg snorted. "Believe it or not, the thought hadn't even crossed my mind, but now that you mention it…." He let the girlfriend remark pass. He wasn't about to burst that particular bubble. Not yet, at any rate.

"Don't you *dare*, Gregory Michael Chambers."

Greg laughed. "I'll call soon, okay? And I'll be sure to call on Christmas Day—if you can tear yourself away from the cooking, or playing with the boys' toys, or—"

"Okay, call over. Take care, sweetheart. Love you."

"Love you too. And give my love to Damon, Tim and Tyler." He disconnected the call and sagged against the cushions. He'd mentioned moving his stuff out as a lighthearted remark, but it did raise a few questions on his mind. At some point, Greg would need to start thinking about his future, a topic he'd put on hold since his dad died. In order to do that, he needed to move on, and that meant…

Opening the box.

Greg knew he'd been putting it off, but perhaps it was finally time.

Greg nudged Micah. "You know what? Your dad isn't as bad at cooking as you had me believe."

Micah smiled. "I hate to disillusion you, but that wonderful lasagna you just ate? Naomi and I made it, then froze it. We just followed Mom's notes." His expression became more wistful. "After she had the tumor removed, she went through a spate of writing down all her recipes. Looking back, it was almost as if she knew what was coming."

"I wish I'd known her. She sounds like she was a wonderful person."

Micah sighed. "Funny. I was thinking just this morning that I wish I'd been able to meet your dad." He sighed. "Don't you think it's weird? Our dads... in love with each other, all those years ago."

"Weird? Maybe. Sad?" Greg stared at the flames in the fireplace. "Things could have been so different."

Micah chuckled. "Yeah. For one thing, you and I might never have existed."

"There *is* that." Greg reflected on his phone conversation that morning, and the thoughts that had been with him ever since. "Could you do me a favor? You know the box on my nightstand?"

Micah stilled. "The one your dad left you?"

Greg nodded. "You think you could fetch it for me?"

He smiled. "No problem." Micah heaved himself up off the couch and left the room. He passed Joshua at the door, who came into the room and went over to the fire to add another log.

"You warm enough?"

Greg laughed. "You've been asking me that all day. And all day you've kept me warm. Thank you."

Joshua smiled. "I wasn't exaggerating about how

cold it gets around here. You haven't seen it, but there's a huge log pile at the side of the house. It's that size for a reason." He glanced up as Micah entered the living room. "Isn't that your box?"

Greg nodded. "And you're just in time for the grand opening." He sighed. "Not that I have a clue what's in it. Dad sealed it before he died."

Joshua came over to the couch and sat beside him as Micah placed the box on Greg's knee. "Do you want to be on your own?" Joshua's voice was kind.

Greg shook his head. "Absolutely not." His heartbeat was racing already; he wanted them with him. Micah sat on the rug in front of the couch, his gaze focused on the box.

Here goes nothing....

Greg found the edge of the cellophane, and began to pull it away from the box. It was a beautiful object, maybe eight inches by five, and under four inches high, covered in intricate carving. Flowers adorned every surface, and in the center of the lid was a tree of life. The box was Indian in appearance, and had a subtle, spicy scent. Greg stared at it, until Micah nudged his good knee.

"It won't open itself, you know," he said softly.

Greg chuckled. "Yeah, I sort of figured that." Slowly he lifted the lid, to reveal a red velvet lining. Two objects lay inside—a folded envelope, and a folded sheet of paper. He stared at the contents. "I wasn't sure what to expect."

Joshua peered into the box. "That looks like a letter."

"Then that's what I'll read first." Greg opened up

the letter and recognized his dad's familiar scrawl. His chest tightened when he saw the date. "Oh wow. He wrote this two days before he died." Micah's hand came to rest on Greg's knee, and he was grateful for the physical contact.

October 10, 2017

Greg,

If you're reading this, then I'm no longer around. I'm not sure how much longer I have left, but I didn't want to leave without sharing a couple of things. 'Leave'—makes it sound like I'm going on a journey, which I suppose I am, in a way. I'm forced to write this when the pain is under control, but before I become too medicated to think clearly.

When you contacted me, I wasn't sure why you wanted to meet me. I'd gotten used to being the absent father who sent cards and gifts, but hung around in the background. I kept things like that for a reason. I know I haven't said much about my life with your mother, but that was down to me entirely. I'll be honest here; I messed up her life. I should never have married her in the first place. Don't get me wrong—I did love her, but it wasn't that earth-shattering, all-consuming love that I knew existed. Ours was more a marriage of two friends, and you were the result. It was when I learned of your impending arrival that I knew I'd made a mistake. I stuck it out for as long as I could, but that wasn't being fair to you or your mother.

Why did I leave? I guess I've left it until right at the last minute because this way, I don't have to look you in the eye when I tell you. The truth is, I've experienced that wonderful love I mentioned just now. I've known what it is to love someone, heart, body and soul. I've also known the heartache and pain of losing that someone. I wish I could see your face now, though. I was so scared to tell you this. So afraid that once everything was out in the open, you'd look at me differently. Because now I know you, son. Well, at least I know more about you. We've not had all that much time to catch up on the last twenty or so years, but it's been enough for me to know you're a good man. So I'm trusting my own judgment here, that you can accept what I'm about to tell you.

I'm gay, son. I knew I was gay when I was fifteen or so, because it was then that I knew I was falling in love with my best friend, Joshua. He loved me too. And but for a quirk of fate, we might have spent the rest of our lives together. It would have been far from where we started our lives, because that wasn't a place where such love would have been tolerated. I wrote Joshua a letter a few months ago, not that I had any intention of mailing it. Except as the end draws closer, I'm rethinking that decision.

What are you thinking as you read these lines? God, I wish I knew.

Funny how life worked out. I left you and your mother, so I could be true to myself, so I could live openly as a gay man. Only, once I'd made the break, once I moved to Wyoming and started a new life… It was so difficult meeting people, stepping out of my comfort zone… I was always a loner when I was younger, and I guess nothing changed. I wish I could say that I lived life to the fullest, but the truth is, once I'd graduated, I threw myself into my work. I did make sure your education was provided for, though. I was so proud of you when you got your MBA. That's going to open so many doors for you.

And that brings me to my last point. When you were born, I took out an insurance policy, naming you as the beneficiary. You'll find the details in the envelope in this box. When you add on the dividends, it doesn't amount to all that much—maybe sixteen thousand dollars—but it's a little something for when you need it. And the house is yours too, to do with as you please. That's all dealt with in my will. You'll find the details of my lawyer in the envelope too. If he hasn't contacted you by now, get in touch with him.

I wish so many things for you—a career that satisfies you, a life that fulfills you… and most importantly, I pray you find someone to love, who loves you with all their heart. Don't make do with anything less than that earth-shattering love, because it does exist, Greg. I hope you find it.

Thank you for being there for me these last few months. You gave me so much strength, and getting to know you was a real privilege. Be happy, son.

Your father.

Greg slowly lowered the letter and gazed at Micah and Joshua, both of whom were regarding him with concern. "I'm okay," he told them, his voice cracking slightly. "There are no new revelations about his life, not after that conversation with my mom and reading his letter to you. But…." He glanced at the letter again, noting how the writing differed from Joshua's letter. The handwriting was spikier, untidier, and he guessed that had something to do with the pain. He picked up the envelope. "He made me beneficiary of an insurance policy, to give me a little capital to start out with. And…." Greg swallowed. "He left me his little house in Jackson."

Something inside him finally broke. His dad was gone.

"I wish I'd told him… that I was gay. I should have." His breathing hitched, and his throat tightened.

"Maybe he knows now," Micah suggested quietly.

There was no way Greg could have stopped the tears after that. Warm, strong arms surrounded him, and he leaned into Joshua, conscious of Micah moving to his other side, yet more strength to support him.

Greg closed his eyes and gave in to his grief, in the knowledge that two men shared it with him.

Chapter Fourteen

"Your face looks better," Naomi commented after she'd been in the house five minutes.

Greg snickered and glanced at Micah. "She doesn't have a filter, does she?"

Micah laughed. "*Now* you're getting it."

Naomi stared at them both. "What's wrong with that? He does look better. All the bruises have gone, and his cuts have healed up." She grinned. "Now we can see how pretty he really is, eh, Micah?"

Greg went all shades of red, and noticeably, his gaze was everywhere but on Micah. Naomi snickered.

Micah was going to swing for her, one of these days. Thankfully, she changed the subject.

"So, is it right what Dad told me on the way here? You're staying for the holidays?"

Greg nodded, his cheeks returning to their normal color. "Looks like you're stuck with me for a while longer." He glanced at his leg. "At least until I can get rid of this cast." He lifted his head to look at them. "Let's hope it's good news on Monday."

"What's happening on Monday?" Naomi asked.

"He goes to the hospital to have his leg X-Rayed," Micah told her. "And he might be taken off the strong painkillers too." He knew the slow progress was getting Greg down.

Joshua came into the living room, his arms full of logs. "One of you give me a hand here, please, before I drop these on my foot?"

Micah dashed over and took logs from his dad's precarious load. "Can't have that. However would we cope if you ended up in a cast? Who'd do the cooking?" Then he grinned. "On second thought...."

Naomi burst out laughing and rushed over to assist. "*I'll* help you, Dad."

"And for your information, I was *about* to drive to Hanks and pick up dinner for all of us." Joshua gazed at Micah with narrowed eyes. "Guess we all know who won't be getting any."

From the couch, Greg started laughing. Micah regarded him quizzically. "And what's tickled you?"

Greg smiled. "I love the way you all interact. No

one would think to hear the way you bicker that you really do love one another."

Joshua stilled. "And I'm glad you can see that, son." He put the remainder of the logs into the basket next to the fireplace, then straightened. "I'll be back soon with dinner." Joshua left the room quickly.

Naomi frowned, staring after him. "Is Dad okay?"

Micah sighed. "Of course he isn't. We're a little closer to Christmas." He put his hand to Naomi's back. "And speaking of which, you might as well get in on the act too." He explained his plan. "Think you can do that?"

She nodded. "Just don't expect miracles. He's not gonna suddenly launch himself into the festive season, you know that, right? Baby steps, Micah."

He nodded. "I was just thinking a tree would be a good start."

"Right now, a good start would be if I do my laundry." Naomi chuckled. "And there's a lot of it."

"Then I'd better empty the washer. I did a load this morning and it's still sitting in there."

"Ew." Naomi wrinkled her nose, before glancing over at Greg. "If I were you, I'd complain when you get your laundry back and it's covered in mold."

Greg laughed. "I'm just grateful he's doing my laundry in the first place. But seeing as most of the clothes I'm wearing are his...."

Naomi grabbed her bag from where she'd dropped it, and headed to the laundry room, Micah following. Once they were inside, she closed the door gently.

Micah arched his eyebrows. "Something up?"

She gave him a sweet smile. "I just don't want him overhearing us, that's all." Naomi put her hands on her hips. "So how are things progressing between you and Greg?"

Micah blinked. "Excuse me?"

Naomi rolled her eyes. "Oh, come *on*. Last time I was home, it was perfectly obvious that you liked him. So... I'm asking. What have you done about it?" She grinned. "Have you kissed him yet?"

"Naomi!" Micah gaped at her. When all he got back was that infuriating grin, he gave up and began tugging the clean clothes from the washer into the basket.

"Good idea." She unzipped her bag. "He can't hear us if the washer is running." She turned the bag upside down, and the dirty clothing tumbled out onto the floor.

Micah shook his head. "Silly me for actually thinking about the clothes, rather than creating a distraction." He did *not* want to talk about this.

Naomi stopped him with a gentle hand on his arm. There was no trace of that grin: warm, deep brown eyes, so like his mom's, gazed back at him. "Talk to me, Micah."

He stared at her in silence, his stomach roiling. "Yes, I like him," he whispered. "But I can't do anything about it."

She frowned. "Why the hell not?"

Micah struggled to find the words. "Because... it feels... bigger than just liking him."

Naomi became very still. "Like... loving him, bigger?"

He nodded, his heart pounding. "Only it's way too soon for it to be love."

Naomi widened her eyes. "According to whose rules?"

"I've known him for four weeks. *Four*. And one of those weeks, he was in the goddamn hospital. You don't fall in love with someone after only four weeks."

"Bullshit," she said bluntly. Then her expression softened. "You remember that movie Mom made us watch every single Christmas? The black and white one, about the guy who gets to find out how much his life impacted on others?"

Micah smiled. "It's A Wonderful Life?"

She nodded, smiling too. "That's the one. Do you recall the scene where George meets Mary at the high school dance? They all fall into the swimming pool? And they end up walking along the street in a bathrobe and football gear?"

"Where are you going with this?" Micah was lost.

"At the end of that scene, they come to this old, deserted house, where everyone usually throws rocks at the windows, or what's left of them, and makes a wish. Mary throws a rock and makes a wish, but we only find out later what that wish was." Naomi smiled. "The night they met, she wished for them to be married, to spend the rest of their lives together. She knew, after only one night."

Micah gave her an indulgent smile. "It's just a movie, sis," he reminded her softly.

Naomi nodded. "And it's Christmas, *bro*. A time for magic and miracles, if ever there was one. For believing in love at first sight. Okay, so it's not *exactly* that here, but you know what I mean." She swallowed.

"I'd like to think I know what Mom would say if she was here."

Micah's throat thickened. "Yeah?"

She bobbed her head slowly. "She'd tell you to follow your heart." Naomi cocked her head to one side. "And what is your heart telling you?"

Micah pulled her into a hug. "That little sisters can be wonderful when they want to be," he whispered. "And that believing in magic is for the movies." He released her, and started shoving the damp clothing into the dryer. "It's easy coming out with all this, but there's one thing your theory doesn't take into consideration." He closed the dryer door with a soft *click*.

"And what's that?"

Micah straightened. "What if Greg doesn't feel for me the way I feel for him?"

Naomi bit her lip. "For an intelligent guy, you come out with some stupid shit." Micah stared at her, and she rolled her eyes. "For God's sake… the way he looks at you. The way he listens to you. Are you really that blind? That deaf? Hell, I saw that the last time I was home."

He had to smile to himself. The irony hadn't escaped him: one look at the photos of Dad and Hayden, and he'd seen their connection, yet he'd failed to see what was under his nose?

If Naomi was correct, of course. And that was a big IF.

"Get your laundry started. I'll go put out the plates. Dad will be home any minute. And we don't want Greg wondering why it takes so long to load a washer, do we?" He left her to it. The truth was, he didn't want to think about the possibility that she might be right.

Life didn't work out like that. There was no such thing as magic, Christmas or otherwise.

Unfortunately.

"Does your mom know you're gay?"

Greg lifted his head from his reading to meet Naomi's direct gaze. "Excuse me?"

Naomi sat up from her reclining position on the rug in front of the fire. "I was talking with Micah after dinner. He said your mom called the other day. I was just wondering if she knew, that's all."

Greg closed his book. "No, she doesn't. I'm not going to share something like that over the phone. But I will tell her. I don't think she'll freak out about it though."

"I see." Naomi drew her knees up to her chest and hugged them. Her long hair gleamed in the firelight as it spilled over her shoulders, reminding him of the portrait. She peered at Joshua, who was sitting in the armchair, staring at his phone. "Dad? How did Mom react when you told her about Hayden? You did say you'd tell us."

"But there's nothing that says he has to tell us *right this second*," Micah said firmly from his position beside Greg on the couch. He gave Naomi a hard stare. "That's surely Dad's decision."

Greg regarded Joshua closely. As much as he liked Naomi, he was prepared to tell her to back off if

Joshua appeared upset by the suggestion. However, Joshua merely nodded.

"I did promise, didn't I?" He placed his phone on the small wooden table beside his chair, then leaned back. "I'm not sure what you're expecting to hear though."

Naomi shifted closer, until she was sat at his feet, gazing up at him. "How did she find out? Did you tell her, or—"

Joshua chuckled. "Here's a novel idea. How about you let *me* tell the story?"

Micah gave Naomi a superior look, and she retorted by giving him the finger. Greg loved Joshua's mock gasp of horror.

"We'd been dating for nearly a year, I suppose. She often came to dinner on the weekend, and my parents adored her. I think a lot of that adoration initially was due to the fact that I was dating a girl." Joshua shook his head. "They spent that whole first year in Wyoming, just… watching me. I felt like I was in prison sometimes. No parties, no after school activities… they didn't trust me."

"That's awful." Naomi scowled. "All because you'd loved a boy?"

Joshua stroked her hair. "Bless you. Times then were nothing like they are now. When you were talking about your classmates the other week, my first thought was how far we've come. Your generation is perhaps the most tolerant yet. Certainly the most accepting. But back then?" He sighed heavily. "Anyhow, I was in the second year at college, and we were coming up on our one-year anniversary. I told your mom I thought it was time we got married."

Micah laughed. "How romantic. I can really feel the love."

"Hush." Naomi glared at Micah. "Let him tell it."

Greg was content just to sit and listen.

"Your mom agreed, and we decided to tell our parents when it got to our anniversary." Joshua stared into the fire. "She said if we were gonna do this, then there had to be no secrets between us. When I asked her what she meant, she got up from her chair, walked over to the shelf above her desk, and took down a book. It was an Agatha Christie I'd loaned her the previous week. I had no idea where she was going with this, until she opened the cover... and took out my photos of Hayden. I must have left them in there, and not noticed when I loaned it to her."

"What did she say?" Micah asked in a low voice.

Joshua met Micah's intense gaze. "She asked me who he was. There was no way I was gonna lie to her. I loved her. So... I told her everything. She just sat there and listened. When I was done, she handed me the book with the photos still in it. She smiled and said, 'I think you'd better put these someplace safe. You don't wanna lose them now, do ya?' I stared at her, and she looked at me like she was puzzled. 'Of course you must keep them. You loved him. I don't think for one second that you'll ever forget him. But I know, with all my heart, that you love me. I guess I'm luckier than Hayden, because I'm the one who gets to keep you.'"

Naomi's mouth fell open. "Way to go, Mom. She knew you were bi, and that didn't change a thing." Her eyes glistened.

Joshua bent over and kissed the top of her head.

"Your mom was an amazing lady, and I will be forever thankful that I had her in my life." The firelight caught the glint in his own eyes. "So now you know."

Greg wished even more that he could have met her. "Thank you for sharing that." His words came out gruffer than he'd intended, and he cleared his throat.

Joshua met his gaze and smiled. "She'd have loved you, son." He glanced at his surroundings, and his face darkened. "And I know she'd have hated this."

Micah jerked his head up. "Hated what?"

Joshua flung his arm out in a sweeping gesture. "When your mom was alive, this room would have been filled with lights and color. Mistletoe hanging over every door, because Lord, that woman loved to sneak up on me with a kiss. A Christmas tree so high, the angel's wings were scraping the ceiling. Now look at it." His face fell. "I step outside into the street, and everywhere I look, there's the lights she loved so much."

"We do understand, Dad," Naomi said softly. "It... hurts us too."

Joshua nodded. "So I've been thinking. If you kids want a tree this year...." He swallowed.

Micah's eyes widened. "For real?" Naomi stared at her dad.

Joshua regarded them both. "Did you want one? Because... I think I can deal with a tree."

Naomi lurched up and flung her arms around Joshua. "Thank you, thank you!"

Joshua chuckled and held her close. "I'm thinking that's a yes." He glanced at Greg. "You like that idea too?"

Greg nodded happily. "I think a tree is a wonderful idea."

"Good. Then you get to go with Micah when he picks it out. You need to get out of the house. That okay with you, Micah?"

Greg loved the glow on Micah's face. "More than okay, Dad." He turned to grin at Greg. "Tomorrow morning, bright and early?"

"Sounds like a plan. Although I won't be able to leave the car, right?"

Micah grinned. "Think again. According to their website, the Home Depot provide motorized carts."

"Motorized—" Joshua narrowed his gaze. "Been doing some research, have we?" His lips twitched.

Micah flushed. "It was just an idea. You know, just in case."

Joshua stared at him for a moment, then erupted into a peal of deep laughter. "Damn, you remind me of your mom sometimes."

Greg thought that was a pretty awesome endorsement.

K.C. WELLS

Chapter Fifteen

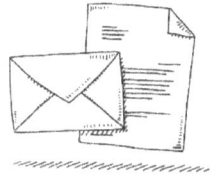

After more than three weeks of being stuck indoors, Greg's senses went into overload. The crisp, cold air on his face, the wonderful scent of the Christmas trees, the luxury of being mobile again.... It was all too much. He stopped the motorized cart at the edge of the tree lot and closed his eyes, turning his face toward the sun.

"I guess it feels like you just got out of prison," Micah said quietly into his ear.

Greg opened his eyes. "You have *no* idea." Getting in and out of Joshua's truck had been awkward, but they'd managed it. And Micah had gone to fetch the cart first, so Greg hadn't had all that far to go. Still, it was a pain not being able to bend his leg, and Greg couldn't wait to be rid of that cast.

Micah eyed the cart. "Are you to be trusted in that thing? I have visions of you mowing down innocent shoppers who can't get out of the way fast enough." His eyes twinkled.

Greg chuckled. "I'm a sensible driver, I'll have you know. Besides, the only person I'll be aiming for is you." He grinned. *How does that saying go? Many a true word is spoken in jest.* Maybe the exhilaration had gone straight to Greg's head: it wasn't like him to flirt. Except... maybe Micah didn't recognize the fact that he was flirting.

Okay, enough innuendos. "Let's go find a tree." He drove onto the lot, conscious of the space between the trees. That heady scent pervaded the air, rekindling memories of Christmas when he was a kid. In later years, Mom had gone down the route of artificial trees, and although they were beautiful, it wasn't the same experience.

Micah strolled beside him. "Basically, we have three types of trees to choose from. I have my own preferences, of course, but seeing as you're the guest, you get to choose."

Greg widened his eyes. "Hey. It's your home. So tell me, what are your thoughts?"

Micah wandered over to the section containing Douglas firs. "These are beautiful, big and bushy, but..."

He fingered a branch. "That's great if all your decorations are nice and light. These branches aren't cut out for anything heavy."

"Agreed. That's a no to Douglas firs then." He moved the cart along to the next section. "And what do we think of Fraser firs?" He liked the silvery blue-green foliage and that perfect Christmas tree shape.

"These are what I always think of when I remember past Christmases." Micah got a faraway look in his eyes. "This was Mom's favorite."

Which was a two-edged sword, in Greg's mind. A continuation of tradition, but bringing with it a wealth of memories, some of them painful.

He sniffed the air. "That smell. Now *that* is Christmas." Greg moved the car around the corner to a huge section, and peered at the label. "Balsam firs." He glanced at Micah. "What do you think?"

Micah gazed at the trees. "I think… we've found our tree. Well, the type anyway. Now to find *our* tree." The way he stressed *our* made Greg's chest tighten. It made the situation sort of… personal, something just for them.

Then he gave himself a mental shake. *Just… stop it*. Such thoughts only served to torment him. It was enough that Micah was already present in Greg's dreams. He didn't need to be thinking about him in his waking hours too. Then he gave an inward snort. He only had to look at Micah, and that was enough to get him thinking.

Greg cleared his throat. "So, how big can we go?" Micah snickered, and Greg rolled his eyes. "When you've finished being a little kid, tell me. Are we talking six feet? Seven? Eight? Ten?"

Micah snorted. "We go home with a ten-foot tree, and Dad will hit the ceiling before the tree has a chance to. Let's stick with eight feet max." He peered into the section. "Wait a sec." Micah dove in and wrestled out a tree, wide at the base, with a fragrance that filled Greg's nostrils. "What about this one?"

Greg beamed. "I like it. Do we need to buy any decorations?" Micah laughed so heartily that Greg started laughing too. "What did I say?"

"Wait until you see all the boxes Dad keeps in the attic. Then you'll know why I'm laughing." He glanced around. "I'll go get someone to net this for us. Oh, and Naomi asked me to buy something else." His cheeks flushed.

Greg was intrigued. "Like what?"

Micah attempted a casual shrug. "She wants some bunches of mistletoe. Said it reminds her of Mom."

Greg tried not to think about it, but no, the thought wormed its way in there. Micah standing below a bough of mistletoe, those soft-looking lips parted, just waiting for a kiss… Greg's kiss.

He coughed. "That's… sweet." Thankfully a guy in coveralls wandered in their direction, and that was an end to the conversation.

Not that it was an end to Greg's thoughts, however.

A CHRISTMAS PROMISE

The living room looked like there'd been an explosion inside a Christmas store, and Micah couldn't have been happier. There were boxes everywhere, garlands lay draped on the couch next to Greg, and every available surface was covered in decorations.

What made it all special was Greg. He demanded to see what was in the boxes, and as each bauble and ornament was removed, Micah and Naomi brought them to him, so he could gaze at them. When it came to placing the decs on the tree, Greg had really come out of his shell, giving instructions on where to put certain pieces. More than once, Naomi had caught Micah's gaze and grinned. It was clear she was loving it too. Dad had insisted on keeping out of the way in his office: he wanted to see the finished result. Micah could understand that. Agreeing to them having a tree was one thing—handling all the decorations that he and Mom had collected over the years? That was something else entirely.

When it became obvious that there wasn't a single part of the tree that wasn't covered, Micah and Naomi stepped back. "You wanna do the honors?" she asked him.

Micah shook his head. "I think we leave that task to Dad."

Naomi nodded. "I'll go get him."

As she walked away, Micah called out, "Wait!" When Naomi stopped and turned, he smiled. "Let's turn on the lights first?"

She nodded and knelt down to reach the wall beside the tree. Seconds later, the room was filled with color, the lights reflecting off the baubles and garlands that festooned the tree. Naomi smiled. "Perfect. *Now* I'll go get him." She walked out of the room.

Micah looked across at Greg. "Well? What do you think?"

Greg's face shone. "It's awesome." He frowned. "What's Joshua going to do?"

Before Micah could answer, Dad came into the room, stopping at his arm chair to stare at the tree. "Oh my."

Naomi joined him at his side. "Do you like it?"

Dad put his arm around her shoulders and squeezed. "It's beautiful, honey." He glanced at Micah. "Well, where is it?"

Micah handed him the last box, and Dad opened it almost reverently. "It still amazes me that this box is still holding together. It was 1991 when we bought it."

From the plain brown carton emerged an angel in a gold and white dress. She held a golden harp, and beautiful gold wings spread out behind her. Her delicate face was painted with a serene expression.

"Oh."

Micah looked at Greg, who was staring at the angel open-mouthed. Micah smiled. "Mom and Dad bought this, their first Christmas together after they got married. It's been on the top of every tree ever since." He watched as Dad climbed up onto the mini step and carefully lowered the angel into position. When he stepped down, his eyes shone.

"She'd love this. You two did great."

"Hey, I helped too!" Greg proclaimed loudly.

Naomi snickered. "Yeah, it was like having Mom here, giving out instructions."

Dad pulled a handkerchief from his pocket and wiped his eyes and nose. "I think I'll go make some hot chocolate. Anyone else want some?" Before they could respond, he left the room.

Naomi's face fell. "I'm sorry. I don't know what came over me. I shouldn't have said that."

"It was fine, honest," Micah reassured her, even though his chest had tightened as soon as the words had left her lips. "You were right, too. That was always Mom's trick." He joined Greg on the couch, and gazed at the tree in front of the window. "It's starting to feel like Christmas."

"Almost." Naomi pointed to the bunches of mistletoe on the coffee table. "I still have to hang these up."

Micah couldn't resist. "You thinking you're gonna get lucky?" He snickered. "I mean, I got you enough to cover every doorway in the house, so if some unlucky guy wanders in, he won't be able to escape."

Naomi flipped him the bird. "Who knows what Santa will have in his sack for me? Maybe a cute hunk, all wrapped up in a big red bow?" She winked. "Want me to put in a good word for you too? That is, assuming you've been nice and not naughty." Her eyes gleamed wickedly.

"I think Micah's always nice," Greg piped up. "And I'm sure Santa will bring him whatever his heart desires."

Micah sighed inwardly. *What I really want is to find you under the tree come Christmas morning, but somehow, I don't think that's about to happen.* Damn Naomi and her talk of Christmas magic. He knew better than to get caught up in such thoughts. They only led to disappointment.

Micah sent up a silent prayer. *Let us just enjoy Christmas? Maybe some peace for Dad, a little joy....*

It wasn't much to ask for, was it?

Fran sat back on her haunches and stared at Greg. "Wanna tell me what's wrong?"

Greg leaned back on his hands and huffed. "Nothing's wrong. Let's just get this over with, all right?" Anything not to extend the torture.

Fran's eyebrows lifted so high, they almost reached her hairline. "Okay," she said slowly. "How about you tell me what they told you at the hospital three days ago? What did the X-Ray show?"

Greg narrowed his gaze. "You already know that, don't you?"

"Maybe." Fran sat beside him on the rug next to his exercise mat, crossing her legs. "Give me your version."

"They said I can manage with over the counter pain stuff now."

She nodded. "And that's good, right?"

"I suppose."

"And the bone's healing?"

Greg sighed. "He said because the break was minor, and because of my age and general health, he was happy with the X-Ray."

"Then what's the problem?"

Greg stared at the cast. "He also said femurs heal very slowly. Not that I hadn't heard *that* before. I asked if I could stand on it yet. He said no, that full healing takes a long time, and that I had to leave it until at least six weeks had passed before I tried putting any weight on it. I still have to wear the damn cast in the shower, and I still have to sit down in there." He hated that feeling of helplessness. Nearly five weeks since he'd been taken to the hospital, and he still couldn't wash himself without sitting down? It was depressing the hell out of him.

"Sweetie, it could be two months before that leg is capable of bearing weight, and you'll still have to use the crutches. I know taking the cast off twice a day to change the dressings is a pain in the neck, because you hate having to put it back on, right?"

He nodded, his heart heavy. It just didn't feel like he was making any progress.

Fran patted his shoulder. "You're doing really well, Greg. I know it doesn't look like it to you, but you are. You're keeping mobile on the crutches, you're doing your exercises…. You just have to be a little patient, that's all."

Greg scowled. "Then I guess we're going to be having this conversation again, because patience is not one of my virtues."

Fran got to her feet. "I think we're done for today." She glanced around the living room. "It sure is looking pretty in here. And that's a great tree. Eleven days to go!"

Despite his mood, Greg had to smile at her gleeful expression. "I bet you have an advent calendar at home, don't you?"

"Two, actually. The hardest part is stopping the boyfriend from opening the one with the chocolates behind the doors. The little shit eats them all!" She held out her hands. "Come on. I'll help you onto the couch. Then you can spend the rest of the day recovering from my torture." Her eyes sparkled with good humor. "Watch a Christmas movie or three. That always puts me in a good mood."

Greg winced as Fran helped him to stand, his left leg off the ground, before she guided him to the couch. He knew once she'd left, he'd head for the shower. Greg was sick and tired of wearing nothing but sweats, something he normally avoided.

I must look like a slob. No wonder Micah isn't interested. It wasn't as if Greg could even catch him under the mistletoe that hung everywhere. Yet another reason to curse his damn leg.

Watching a movie was a bad idea. Right then Greg wasn't good company for anyone. Better to stay in his room and read, where he wouldn't be tempted to stare at Micah and torture himself with dreams that might never come true.

Chapter Sixteen

Micah had no idea what was going on with Greg, but it felt like a backwards step. He'd spent all day in his room, only surfacing to eat or go to the bathroom. Even Dad had noticed. He kept glancing toward Greg's door, his brow furrowed. Naomi had suggested going to talk to him, but Micah shook his head.

"He obviously needs some time on his own."

Naomi frowned. "I don't get it. He was fine at the weekend when we decorated the tree."

Micah had a theory. "I think he's depressed." Just the thought made him ache inside.

Dad put down his phone and stared at him. "What's getting him down? I know we haven't known him all that long, but this seems out of character, somehow."

"I saw his therapist just before she left this morning. She didn't look happy. Maybe his leg is bothering him."

"And maybe what he needs is cheering up," Naomi said firmly.

Dad peered at her. "I know that tone. You're up to something." He smiled. "You got a plan?"

She nodded. "How about we all put on our coats and jackets, get into Micah's car, and take Greg to see the Festival of Lights? That would bring a smile to anyone's face."

"Why my car?"

Naomi rolled her eyes. "Because you could push the passenger seat back so Greg could sit up front with his leg straight. I'm only little. I could squeeze in behind him."

"Maybe you kids should go," Dad said after a moment. "You don't need me with you."

"Maybe we'd *prefer* to have you with us." Naomi met his gaze. "Come on, Dad. It'll be fun."

"Maybe we should find out if Greg wants to go first?" Micah said with a wry smile. "That is the point of the trip, right? To cheer up Greg?"

Naomi bit her lip, and Dad chuckled. "Good point. Go see if he likes the idea."

Micah went up to Greg's door, and rapped gently on it.

"Come in."

Greg was sitting on his bed, propped up by a heap of pillows. He was fastening the Velcro straps on his cast as Micah stepped into the room. He looked up as Micah approached. "Hey." He sounded cheerful enough, but Micah wasn't fooled: Greg's smile didn't reach his eyes.

"Listen, there's something we'd like to do this evening, and we want you to join us."

Greg arched his eyebrows. "Sounds intriguing."

"We're all going to the Festival of Lights. Would you come?"

After a moment's hesitation, Greg shook his head. "Thanks for asking, but I don't think that would be a good idea. I'm not exactly good company right now."

"Aw. I was hoping you'd say yes. Dad was really looking forward to you coming with us," Micah lied. It was only a tiny white lie, after all, and if it worked, then it didn't count as a lie. He smiled to himself at the almost childlike reasoning.

Greg stilled. "Really?"

Micah nodded, sensing capitulation. "It was mine and Naomi's idea. After the tree worked so well, we thought we'd try a little nudge in a positive direction. I sort of told Dad you wanted to come too, and his face lit up. You wouldn't wanna disappoint him now, would you?" Okay, that was an outright lie, but Micah was past caring. He really wanted Greg to come along.

Greg sighed. "When you put it like that? No, I wouldn't. When were you thinking of going?"

"Er, now, actually."

Greg stared at him, then rolled his eyes. "Fine.

Could you grab my jacket? It's in the closet, along with my boots."

"Sure. I'll give you a hand to put them on too." Micah darted into the closet and grabbed the jacket off its hanger. Inwardly he was grinning. *Yes!*

It wasn't until he was helping Greg into the front seat that he realized just how much this meant to him.

Micah glanced in the rear-view mirror. "We all okay back there?"

"No, *we* are not," Naomi said pointedly. "I can hardly move. My legs are squashed up against the seat."

"I've got plenty of room," Dad said, smirking. "It's only a forty-five-minute trip. What are you complaining about? Just think about what's at the other end." He caught Micah's gaze in the mirror and grinned.

What the hell? Dad agreeing to go to the lights in the first place was enough of a shock. His enthusiasm was nothing short of perplexing.

Naomi cleared her throat. "You're right. I can put up with a little discomfort. What's forty-five minutes?"

Right then Micah wished he could see Naomi's face, because that didn't sound like his sister at all. And judging by the whispers and chuckles coming from the back seat, she and his dad were up to something.

"Well, what are you waiting for? Santa's reindeer to come pull us there?" Dad snickered. "Let's go!"

Now Micah was certain they were up to something.

Micah switched off the engine. "There's a bus ride that takes you all through the park," he told Greg. "That way, you get to see everything."

Greg smiled. "I saw plenty coming in." It wasn't as though you could miss the park: brightly lit signs pointed the way all along the highway. There had been one heart-stopping moment before they'd turned right off South Douglas Highway onto Garner Lake Road: just after the turn, Greg spotted Jake's Tavern, and the sight had been enough to send cold shivers down his spine.

Then Micah reached across and found Greg's hand. He squeezed it gently, and Greg breathed a little easier.

"Naomi was right. This is just what you need to banish the blues," Joshua said, unbuckling his seatbelt.

Greg blinked and turned his head to stare at Micah.

"Dad? Let's go wait by the fire for the next bus. Micah, you and Greg stay in the car. Greg can't stand anyway, so we'll come get you when the bus comes in, okay?" Naomi all but pushed Joshua out of the car. They walked rapidly across the lot to the firepit, where several people were already waiting, stamping their feet and warming their hands on the flames.

Greg cleared his throat. "Just what *I* need to banish the blues, huh?" He was trying not to laugh.

Micah couldn't lie his way out of this: Joshua had let the cat out of the bag.

Micah coughed. "Okay, so I may have twisted the truth a little, but Dad's right. You needed this."

"So all that about doing a little more to get your dad in the Christmas spirit… that was bullshit, right?" Greg shook his head. "You didn't tell Joshua I wanted to come, did you? This was all a ruse to get me out of my room."

"Not just you—my dad too." Micah heaved a sigh. "Look, I'm sorry. You seemed so low, and I couldn't bear to see you like that. Then Naomi came up with this stupid plan, and I—"

"I never said it was stupid," Greg blurted out. His heartbeat raced. "I think it was a great idea. Now tell me why it was so important that I came too." He prayed it wasn't merely altruism on Micah's part. Not that.

"I…." Micah took a deep breath, opened his mouth to speak, then snapped it shut.

Greg wanted to scream. Instead, he changed the subject. "The lights *are* beautiful." The glimpses he'd gotten as they drove into the park had brought back a sense of childlike wonder.

"They are," Micah agreed, "but there's something here more beautiful than any of the displays."

"And what's that?"

"You."

Greg's breath caught in his throat. "What?"

Micah smiled. "You heard me."

"I did, but I seem to be having trouble believing it." Because it sounded to Greg like—

The creak of leather as Micah shifted in his seat,

a gentle hand cupping Greg's cheek, then two lips brushed against his. Greg breathed in Micah's scent, the fragrance that still clung to his hair from the shower he'd taken, and the merest hint of spicy cologne. The kiss was tender, deliberate, and set his pulse racing. Micah's fingers traced the contours of his face, and still he kissed Greg, his lips warm and silky.

Micah broke the kiss and pulled back to gaze at him. "Now do you believe me?" he murmured.

Greg smiled, his heart dancing. "I think I may need a little more proof."

Micah's grin sent warmth flooding through him. "I can provide that." And before Greg could utter another word, Micah's fingers caressed his neck as he brought their mouths together in another languid kiss. This time Greg closed his eyes and gave himself up to the intimate connection, his hands on Micah's head and shoulder, letting out a tiny noise of contentment when Micah's tongue parted his lips. Greg opened for him without reservation, sighing inwardly when Micah made low noises of approval.

As first kisses went, this was sublime.

Slowly, Micah drew back, his breathing slightly faster. "We'd better stop, or we'll miss the bus to see the lights."

Greg opened his eyes wide. "There are lights?"

A tap on the window made them both jump. Naomi was grinning at them through the window.

"Do you think she saw anything?" Greg said in a low voice.

Micah snorted. "I'm starting to think she engineered the whole situation from the beginning."

Naomi was looking pretty smug. He opened the window. "Yes?"

"The bus is here," she said, her grin not diminishing in the slightest. "Unless you two want to catch the next one? Dad and I wouldn't mind if you wanted to be alone." She batted her lashes.

"God, you're insufferable when you're smug." Micah closed the window and turned to Greg. "Ready for a bus ride?"

"As long as we continue this... conversation when we get home." Greg didn't want to lose this gloriously happy feeling.

"I promise." Micah leaned in quickly and kissed Greg on the lips. "A little more proof," he said with a smile. "Now let's go stare at the pretty lights that can't hold a candle to you."

Greg waited for Micah to come around to his side of the car, to help him. All the while, his head was in a whirl.

Micah kissed me.

Greg wasn't entirely sure who to thank—God, or Santa.

"I'm bushed. I'm going to bed." Naomi kissed Micah on the cheek. "Sweet dreams. I don't have to guess who'll be in them, right?"

Micah grabbed her arm before she could walk

away. "Okay, truth time." Greg was in the bathroom and Dad was in his office. "Did you plan that?"

Naomi gave him a wide-eyed stare. "Plan what?"

Micah snorted. "You haven't been able to pull off innocent for years, so don't even try. That whole trip to see the lights—leaving Greg and me alone in the car— was that all part of a plan? And if it was, how much did Dad know?" He still couldn't believe how quickly Dad had agreed to the trip in the first place.

Naomi glanced down to where he still held her arm. Micah let go, and she sighed. "I just felt you two needed a little push in the right direction. It meant leaving a lot to chance, that you'd actually get up enough nerve to kiss him, but I figured with the romantic setting, the odds were in my favor."

"You… conniving, scheming, manipulative little—"

"But to answer your question," she interjected. "Yes, Dad knew. When you went to ask Greg, I took Dad aside and told him I thought you and Greg were interested in each other. I said all you needed was a little time on your own, in the right setting. He said go for it."

"Dad… approved of your matchmaking?"

She smiled. "Micah, he really, *really* likes Greg. I do too. I think you're perfect for each other. The only ones who couldn't see it were you two." She leaned into him and hugged him. "Is it so hard to believe that we just want you to be happy?" Then she straightened. "So if we're done, I'm going to bed. Just one last thing." Her eyes gleamed. "I made certain there was plenty of mistletoe around here. At least *try* to get some use out of it?" And with that, she darted out of the kitchen, her shoulders shaking with laughter.

Micah stared after her, stunned.

From behind him, Dad cleared his throat. "I think I'll go off to bed too. It's been a long day." He patted Micah on the back. "Don't stay up too late." Dad poured himself a glass of water and went to leave the kitchen.

No way was Micah about to let him off *that* easily. "That's it? That's all I get?"

Dad came to a halt and turned slowly to face him. "Since the day you told me and your mom that you were gay, I've been waiting for you to bring someone home to meet us. All the way through college, we wondered if you'd met someone, but were too shy to bring him home. When you graduated, and still there was no one, we told ourselves it was good that you weren't rushing into anything. When the Supreme Court ruled in 2015, your mom was overjoyed. She said she was gonna live to see both our kids married." His face tightened. "Yeah, well… What I'm trying to say here is…." He drew in a deep breath. "I just want you to be happy. And tonight, when I saw you and Greg together…." Dad smiled. "You looked happy," he said simply.

Micah chuckled. "Dad, that was our first kiss. Don't go making wedding plans just yet, okay?"

"But you do like him?" Dad gazed at him steadily.

Micah sighed. "It's more than like. I still need to find out where he stands."

"Then stop talking to me, and go talk to Greg!" Dad shook his head. "To quote a line from one on your mom's favorite movies… youth is wasted on the wrong people." Muttering under his breath, he went to his room.

Micah waited until the house was quiet. There was no sign of Greg, so Micah figured he was in his room. He turned off the lights everywhere and was about to head that way, when something caught his eye. Micah grinned. Seeing as Naomi had gone to so much trouble....

He knocked quietly on Greg's door.

"Come in."

Micah stuck his head around it. Greg was lying on his bed, arms folded behind his head. He smiled at Micah. "I was just thinking about you."

"I haven't come empty-handed." Micah held up the sprig of mistletoe.

Greg's smiled widened. "In that case, you'd better get in here."

"I was hoping you'd say that." Micah entered Greg's bedroom and closed the door quietly behind him.

Chapter Seventeen

Greg patted the bed beside him. "Sit here, there's plenty of space." It took him a moment to realize he was nervous. When they arrived home after the trip to the lights, he'd wanted to take Micah aside and talk to him, only the timing wasn't right. For one thing, he was conscious of Naomi's scrutiny, not to mention Joshua's glances. Greg had so many questions he wanted to ask, but he guessed they'd have to wait for a more opportune time.

He hadn't figured on Micah taking matters into his own hands.

Micah came around the bed, but instead of sitting, he stretched out on his side, his head propped up on his hand, his gaze focused on Greg, the sprig of mistletoe on the bed between them.

Greg had had more than enough scrutiny for one night. "So, were you right? Was this whole evening part of some scheme of Naomi's?"

Micah laughed, nodding. "She involved my dad too."

Greg blinked. "No kidding."

"Yeah. We talked just now in the kitchen. Dad made me realize you and I have some talking to do of our own."

That was the opening Greg was looking for. "How about we start with that kiss?" His heartbeat sped up at the memory of Micah's lips pressed against his. "Was that an out-of-the-blue thing, or had you been thinking about it for a while? Because you sure took me by surprise."

Micah sighed. "I didn't plan it, but... yeah, I've been thinking about it for a while."

"You... you have?"

"I guess I held back, because... you were hurting, there was so much going on...." Micah smiled. "I'm assuming you didn't mind."

"Wasn't it obvious?" Greg took a deep breath. "You've set the bar very high, you know."

"What do you mean?"

"That was my first kiss from a guy."

Micah's eyes widened. "Really?"

Greg nodded. "It'll take a lot to beat that." Not that he wanted anyone else, but Micah didn't need to hear that right then. There was no way Greg was going to scare him like that.

"I had no idea."

Greg chuckled. "I only came out at Thanksgiving, remember?"

Micah nodded slowly. "Your epiphany. You did say you'd tell me. Well, now is as good a time as any."

Greg had had the same thought. "It only struck me a few weeks ago that my dad and I weren't so different. We were both loners. And I never really had girlfriends to speak of, but it never bothered me. I always assumed I'd know when I met the right person. So there I was, in the last year of my MBA, and I was finally dating someone. Her name was Caroline. She was a sweet girl, intelligent, and good company. We were… comfortable with each other, I guess."

"What happened to change that?"

"We were at her place, and we were kissing on her couch. Well, after five minutes or so, Caroline just… stopped. I did too, thinking something was wrong. I mean, I'd never made out with anyone before, but I didn't think I'd overstepped any boundaries. Anyhow, she stared at me for a minute or so, and then she said the oddest thing." He could still hear her words in his head. "She smiled and said, 'You're not really into this, are you?' I wasn't sure whether I should be insulted or relieved. She was right, of course. I didn't feel…anything, and I was horrified that it had been that obvious."

Micah laid a hand on his chest, and Greg welcomed its warmth, the connection between them.

"Then she peered at me and said, 'Do you think you might be gay?' I guess my jaw dropped, because she smiled and said, 'Not that there's anything wrong with that. But maybe you're more attracted to men than women.'"

"You'd never considered it before then?" Micah asked.

Greg shook his head. "Like I said, I kept to myself. I had a few friends, sure, but I wasn't attracted to any of them. But once she'd said that, it got me thinking. Was she right? *Was* I gay? I spent the following weeks analyzing every look I got, every time I noticed a guy. I had to admit in the end that it was a possibility. Not that I took any steps to *prove* that theory, one way or another."

"Then what happened?"

Greg smiled. "Nothing. No guys suddenly crawled out of the woodwork. I didn't fall hopelessly in love with anyone. I wasn't even remotely attracted to anyone. I got on with my life. I finished my studies, and that was when I learned about my dad's diagnosis. I packed a suitcase, and told my mom I was going to stay with him. No way was I going to let him be alone. Job hunting could wait." It hadn't been an easy time, but he'd shared enough heartache with Micah: he wasn't about to share even more.

"I think that was awesome," Micah said softly. "What did your dad die from?"

"Pancreatic cancer." Greg swallowed. He'd been in so much pain. "When he'd gone, I stayed for a month in his house. I didn't do a great deal, mainly sleeping and reading. I knew I'd have to return to reality at some point. The funeral had taken place, but I was in no hurry to go home. As for the letter…" He sighed. "I could have stuck it in a mailbox. Much simpler that way. After all, I'd found your dad's address. But something inside kept gnawing away at me, and I decided to deliver it in person. By that point, I'd just about run out of money, so hitchhiking was the only option. I wasn't that concerned: Wright was only nine or ten hours away. And the rest you already know."

"Not quite." Micah stroked his chest. "I told you I'd been wanting to kiss you a while ago. But when I kissed you tonight… you wanted it too, didn't you?"

Greg nodded. It was a relief to be able to say what had been on his heart these last few weeks. "It didn't take me long to realize I had a crush on you, so I guess I finally had my answer. Then when you kissed me…" He smiled. "That was all the proof I needed."

Micah grinned. "Yup. Definitely gay."

Greg picked up the mistletoe. "I suppose we should see if this works. I mean, it might be defective." His heart hammered, and his breathing sped up.

"Absolutely." Micah took it from him and held it above their heads. "So how does this work again?" He was smiling.

"Something like this." Greg cupped the back of Micah's head and pulled him down into a kiss, not bothering to hold back from the pleasure he now knew was to be found when those lips met his. Micah shifted closer, his chest on Greg's, the mistletoe dropping onto the bed as he explored Greg's mouth, his tongue pushing deep inside. Greg moaned softly and stroked Micah's back, cursing his inability to move the way he wanted.

And then he had to go and yawn. "Oh my God, I'm so sorry. That wasn't a comment on your technique, honest." *Who the hell yawns mid-kiss?*

"That's a relief." Micah chuckled and pulled back. "It's okay, really. I think the trip wore you out. And it *is* getting late. Maybe we should postpone this until we've both had some sleep."

Greg had no problem with that whatsoever. It wasn't that he didn't want things to move on apace, but he had to admit he was nervous about the prospect. "Sounds good to me." He kept his voice even.

Micah widened his eyes. "Oh my God. It's only just sunk in."

"What?"

He smiled, his eyes kind. "What you were saying, about dating… You're a virgin."

Greg swallowed. "And is that a problem?"

Micah moved slowly, like molasses in winter, until his lips were inches from Greg's. "Not for me. And I'm in no hurry, all right?"

Something eased inside Greg, and he shuddered out a breath. "Thank you." He knew he needn't have worried: he trusted Micah. And then he gave himself up to a slow, tender kiss that made his toes curl and sent warmth surging through his body.

"Good night," Micah murmured against his lips, before finally pulling back and climbing off the bed. "Sleep well." He smiled. "And sweet dreams." Micah walked toward the door.

"Only if you're in them," Greg flung back at him.

Micah paused and turned to look at him. "Then I'll have to see what I can do about that." He left the room, closing the door quietly behind him.

Greg stared at it, still processing the night's events. *He kissed me. He's interested in me. He fucking wants me.* That last part was a bit of a leap, but the implication was certainly there, especially after his comment about Greg's virginity not being a problem.

Greg suddenly knew *exactly* what he wanted to dream about. The only drawback was the lack of lube. A licked palm wasn't ideal, but it was better than nothing.

I think I need to go shopping.

Greg put the phone down and sat back in Joshua's chair, smiling. "Well, it looks like I'll be in the black again soon."

From the couch, Joshua glanced up. "It all sounded very straightforward."

Greg nodded. The lawyer had been expecting his call, just like Dad had explained in his letter. "He's emailing me a document to sign, then the funds will be deposited in my bank account by the end of next week. And he says the deeds to the house are already in my name: Dad saw to that before he died."

Joshua smiled. "A man of property. What will you do with it? Will you live in it, or sell it?"

Greg gazed at him. "If I'm honest? Right now, I have no idea. I can't think beyond getting this cast off my leg. I know I need to think about job applications, but it's not as if I'm going to attend any interviews like this, right?" He gestured to his leg.

"I'd also guess you have no idea where you'll end up," Joshua added. "I mean, you could go back to California, right?" He leaned forward. "If you wanted to, of course. I don't know, maybe there are other factors to consider."

Greg didn't need to be a genius to read between the lines. Joshua wasn't talking about Greg's job prospects—he was thinking of Micah. Hell, if he'd seen them last night, he knew things had changed a little. Well, more than a little. He could hear Joshua's unspoken question, clear as day; *Are you going to leave and break my son's heart?*

For one thing, Greg didn't believe Micah's heart was that fragile. For another, right then he had *no freaking idea* where this was going. He couldn't reassure Joshua because he wasn't going to make promises he couldn't keep.

"I'm not about to make any vital decisions just yet," Greg said truthfully. "Right now, my goals are to get rid of this cast, walk without these crutches, and get my life back to some semblance of normality." He smiled. "That's not so much to ask, is it?"

"Those are good goals," Joshua agreed. "Plus, you get to enjoy a Wyoming Christmas." He grinned. "Without the turkey feathers."

Greg laughed and wiped his brow in exaggerated relief. Then he had an idea. "If I'm financially solvent by the end of next week, I'd like to do a little shopping."

Joshua frowned. "I'm not so sure about that."

"I'll go online first, and do some research, so I can spend as little time on my feet as possible. First item on the list will be a new phone, because it's been hell being without mine. And I *will* be buying gifts for you and your family, so you'd better get used to the idea." Greg set his jaw.

"Lord, another stubborn one." Joshua smiled. "We'll see what we can arrange, okay?"

That sounded positive. "Okay." After the way they'd taken him in, cared for him… Greg wanted to show them how much he appreciated everything they'd done. Not that a few gifts would suffice, but how did the saying go?

It's the thought that counts.

Monday morning, and the house was quiet. Dad and Naomi had gotten up early and had gone to Gillette to shop for groceries. Micah had a suspicion Naomi also wanted to do a little gift shopping, so heaven knew when they'd be back. Greg hadn't surfaced yet, although Micah had heard the faint noise of running water, so evidently, he'd gotten as far as the bathroom.

Micah added logs to the fire and then switched on the tree lights. Every time he glanced at the beautiful tree, he sent up a prayer of gratitude. He'd never expected his dad to take such a step. Micah could only guess at the profundity of his dad's grief, but he knew it would take a long time for the rawness of his pain to dull even a little.

Micah sat in the armchair, warming himself by the fire. The sound of Greg's shower filtered through, a soothing noise, and he leaned back, closing his eyes. What came to mind was a naked, wet, soapy Greg, and Micah went with it, conjuring up a steamy bathroom, roaming hands, warm, wet kisses, and….

He sat upright, eyes open. *Okay. It has been* way *too long since I got laid.* Not that this was the first time he'd thought of Greg in such terms. Five days since that first kiss, and there had been more, mostly when no one was around. In the studio, in Greg's room before they said goodnight, whenever they got the chance. It was weird. Naomi and Dad had seen them that night, but that didn't mean Micah wanted an audience, especially when it comprised of his dad and sister.

Ew. Just… no.

"Micah?" Greg's voice was faint.

Micah dashed to the bathroom door. "Are you okay?"

"That depends. Are your dad and Naomi still out?"

Micah arched his eyebrows at the odd question. "Er, yeah."

"Then… would you like to come in here and wash my back?"

Micah had to smile at that. "Wash your back? Really?"

"Oh, get your butt in here."

Micah chuckled and tried the handle. The door wasn't locked, so he pushed it open. A glass partition closed off the end of the small room, creating a walk-in shower, with a bench at one end. Greg was sitting there, leaning against the tiles, his leg stretched out in front of him, swathed in plastic. In one hand he held the shower head. He smiled, but the rise and fall of his chest revealed his nerves.

What surprised Micah was that Greg wasn't the only one. Micah's heartbeat sped up, and disconcertingly, his dick reacted too. Slowly, he walked over to the glass,

Greg's gaze not breaking contact once. "I suppose, if I'm going to wash your back, I'd better get rid of these clothes."

Greg smirked. "Okay, that sounds really cheesy. Like something out of a really bad porno."

Micah raised his eyebrows. "And you'd know this how?" He grinned.

Greg rolled his eyes. "Duh. How old am I? And you're still dressed." Despite his nonchalance, that bob of his Adam's apple betrayed him.

Micah could help with that.

He pulled his sweater up and over his head, then his T-shirt was next. Greg watched him intently, his only movement when he hung the shower head on the wall. Micah removed his socks, and straightened. By now his cock was already pushing at his zipper—

And Greg noticed. He glanced down at Micah's crotch and swallowed.

Micah unbuttoned his jeans and slid the zipper lower, revealing the base of his thickening dick. *Of all the days to go commando...* He caught the hitch in Greg's breathing, but deliberately avoided his gaze as he pushed down his jeans, his cock rising, pointing in Greg's direction like a goddamn homing beacon. His clothing kicked aside, Micah stepped into the shower and stood in front of Greg, grateful for the warm, moist air.

He figured this was not the time for playing coy. Micah reached for his own dick and pumped it, keeping his movements unhurried. Greg's gaze met his, and he drew in a deep breath.

Micah gave him a reassuring smile, his fingers curled around his shaft, giving it another slow tug.

Greg had his crotch covered with one hand, but

as Micah watched, he lowered it, revealing his half-hard dick. Micah's breathing sped up. "Is that for me?"

Greg swallowed again. "Possibly."

Micah's gaze flicked up to Greg's face. "Only possibly?" he teased.

"Well, it depends. If you're only going to *look* at it, then...."

Micah stepped forward and knelt on the tiles in front of him. He kept his eyes focused on Greg's as he slid his hand down Greg's slick torso until his fingers met the damp curls above his cock.

Greg shivered. "Don't stop there."

Micah traced along the length of his dick with a single finger, until he met the stickiness of Greg's pre-come. Greg's lips parted, and a soft noise escaped as Micah brought the finger to his own tongue.

"Tastes sweet," he whispered, before bracing one hand on Greg's right thigh and wrapping his fingers around Greg's now rigid cock. Micah leaned forward and took Greg into his mouth. Greg shuddered, his hands going to Micah's head, grabbing onto Micah's hair as he pushed deeper, his body trembling.

Micah pulled free and grinned at him. "Sit still, or I stop."

Greg groaned, but nodded. "Just so you know? This is gonna be over real soon."

"Then I'd better make it good."

Another shudder rippled through Greg as Micah sucked on the head of his cock, swirling his tongue around the ridge, before swallowing and taking his shaft into his throat.

"Oh, Christ!" Greg stiffened, his hands returning to grasp Micah's head. That was all the warning Micah got, before warm come pulsed into his mouth, Greg shaking and gasping with every throb of his dick. Micah drank it all down, his hand rubbing Greg's thigh, moving higher to stroke his balls. When he was sure there wasn't a drop left, he licked Greg's cock from head to root, before kissing it tenderly. Then he kissed up Greg's body until their mouths met. Greg wrapped his arms around Micah and held onto him as Micah explored him.

When they parted, Greg sighed. "Wow. That was even better than I'd imagined it would be."

Micah smiled and kissed the tip of his nose. "And one day when we're not in a shower, you get to do the same to me."

Greg's eyes gleamed. "Yes, please. But are you sure about the not-in-the-shower part?" His gaze flickered down to Micah's erection.

Micah grinned. "You can't even stand, let alone suck me off. So no, not this time. But don't worry. I have plans for this." He stood up and tugged on his aching dick. "I get to come all over your chest, and you get to wash it all off." He nodded toward the bottle of body wash. "And then I get to wash your back. That *is* what I'm here for, right?"

Greg laughed. "Of course." He cocked his head to one side, and paled. "Oh, shit."

Micah groaned. Greg had heard right. "Damn their timing." His boner would have to wait. "You stay here. I'll go to my room and dry off there." He stepped out onto the bathmat and grabbed a towel from the rail. He wrapped it around him and hastily picked up his heap of clothing. Micah went over to the door and listened. "They're in the kitchen, I think," he whispered. Slowly and quietly, he opened the door, and—

Dad was standing outside the bathroom, arms folded, grinning. "Conserving water, are we?"

From the kitchen, Micah caught Naomi's groan. "Dad. You are so mean."

Dad snickered. "Only because I wouldn't let you be the one to catch them." His eyes twinkled. "Need some clean clothes, Micah?"

Micah rolled his eyes. "I swear, you two…" He gave his dad a stern glance and lowered his voice. "You do *not* tease him about this, all right? That would *not* be cool." Greg would be mortified.

Dad's expression changed instantly. "Gotcha. We'd never get him to leave his room again." He widened his eyes. "It was Naomi's idea."

"Hey, don't you go throwing *me* under the bus!" Naomi yelled.

Micah shook his head. "You're as bad as each other." He waited until his dad had gone back to start arguing with Naomi, before sticking his head around the bathroom door. "Come out whenever you want. And don't mind them."

Greg was already drying himself off. He grinned. "Don't you worry about me. I can give as good as I get."

Micah liked this new, confident Greg. "I don't doubt it."

Greg gave him a warm smile. "I'm guessing this is another postponement?"

Micah chuckled. "Count on it." Only next time, he'd make sure there were no interruptions.

Chapter Eighteen

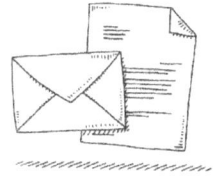

"You know it's going to be crazy today, right?" Micah said as he switched off the engine. "I mean, who in their right mind goes Christmas shopping the day before Christmas Eve? And on a Saturday too?"

Greg snorted. "My mom used to go out on Christmas Eve, after about three o'clock. She said by then, all the stores were getting ready for the post-Christmas sales, and she could grab some real bargains."

Micah stared at him. "Seriously? Tell me she didn't drag you along with her."

Greg laughed. "Only if I was *really* unlucky. Damon hated shopping with a passion, so she'd leave him at home with me. And we're only doing this now because I finally have the money to do it."

Micah sighed. "Yeah, I get that, but there are going to be tons of people shopping today. And what if there are no motorized carts around here?"

Greg had already considered that. He'd looked up Powder Basin Shopping Center online, but hadn't been able to find any mention of such a thing. "Then we take things nice and slow, all right? I don't have that much to buy, and if I—or you, for that matter—think I'm getting tired, then we pull the plug. Agreed?"

"Agreed." Then Micah smiled, leaned over and kissed him.

"What was that for?" Greg loved how Micah's kisses always made him feel warm inside.

Micah arched his brows. "I need a reason now to kiss you?" He grinned. "Am I on your Christmas list?"

"Well, that depends." Greg kept his face straight. "Have you been a good little boy?"

Micah's smile grew wicked and he brushed his lips against Greg's ear. "I recall you saying last night that I was very good. Mind you, I *did* have your dick in my mouth at the time, so that may have influenced your decision a tad."

Okay, now Greg was hot. He cleared his throat, trying his utmost to avoid adjusting himself. "Your timing sucks, you know that, right?"

Micah snorted. "You said sucks."

"How old are you—twelve?" Greg rolled his eyes. "Okay, let's get this show on the road." First stop was to buy a phone, then he had two stores he wanted to visit, so he had at least one gift each for Naomi and Joshua. He wasn't going to buy Micah's gift, not with him right there. Joshua was taking care of that task for him.

"Where first?"

Greg pulled out his phone and consulted his notes. "Phone first, then Heaven to Earth. Wherever that is."

"That's okay, I know it." Micah cocked his head. "But what are you going there for?" Then he held up his hands. "None of my business."

Greg chuckled. "Something for your dad. And you'll laugh when you see it." He leaned back and grabbed his crutches, knowing that Micah would be there to help him out of the car. If there were no carts, he'd be leaning on Micah a lot that morning.

Not that that was such a bad thing.

Greg knew when he was beaten. He was dog tired, his leg ached, and he was starving to boot. "Is there anywhere around here where we can get something to eat?" Micah was carrying his bags: no way could Greg manage them *and* his crutches. It was looking like he'd badly underestimated how tiring the shopping trip would be, or the toll it would take.

Micah took one glance at his face and scowled.

"Why didn't you say something earlier? You look like you're about to fall over right this second."

The last thing Greg wanted was Micah worrying about him. "I'm a little tired, but I really am hungry."

Micah nodded. "Then we're going to Perkin's, just across the parking lot. If you can make it that far, or do I need to fetch the car?" He gave Greg a hard stare. "Just how tired are you?"

Greg sighed. "Okay, so you can stick a fork in me. Happy now? As soon as we've eaten, we can go home. I've got everything I came for." He caught the brief flash of surprise on Micah's face. Micah couldn't have missed the fact that Greg had bought gifts for Naomi and Joshua, but nothing for him. Greg had already shopped online for his family, although they'd receive them a little late.

Don't worry, honey. I've not forgotten you. Greg hoped Joshua had been successful.

Micah pointed behind them. "It's this way."

Carefully, Greg hobbled in the direction of the restaurant, Micah keeping pace with him, watching anxiously. Greg knew he'd be a lot better off once he was able to sit a while. When they got into the crowded restaurant, a server showed them to a table, and finally he could take the weight off. He stood his crutches against the wall of the booth and sagged against the padded back of the bench, his leg stretched out in front of him.

Micah handed him a menu. "I just want a quick bite. I want to get you home."

Greg had no problems with that whatsoever.

By the time the server had taken their orders and he'd drunk a glass of water, he was feeling a little better.

It must have showed in his face, because Micah smiled. "You've got your color back."

Greg nodded. "I'll feel even better when I get a turkey and avocado BLT inside me. Although I *might* sneak a bite of your roast beef and swiss cheese."

Micah's eyes glittered. "And I *might* let you."

Just then their server turned up with two full plates, and all conversation was forgotten for ten minutes or so. Greg attacked his sandwich with gusto, and devoured every one of his fries. Another glass of water, and he was feeling human again. He relaxed, listening to the excited chatter around him, children talking animatedly about Christmas.

I remember being that age. I couldn't wait for Christmas morning.

Then he stiffened. Ice crawled sluggishly through his veins and an invisible iron band around his chest constricted his breathing.

"Greg?" Micah leaned across the table, reaching for his hand. "My God, you're as white as that table top. What's wrong?"

Greg was trembling. Slowly, keeping his head facing forward, he leaned toward Micah. "Behind me," he whispered. "Are there two guys sitting nearby? Just two guys at a table?"

Micah looked beyond him. "Yeah. They're about two tables away from us." He gripped Greg's hand tightly. "What is it?"

Greg swallowed hard. "They're the two men who attacked me." He still heard their voices from that night, each time they invaded his dreams.

Micah gaped. "Are you sure?"

Greg nodded. "I'd know those voices anywhere. I can't turn around though. I just can't." One look at those guys and he'd break, he knew it. "Does one of them have a reddish beard? Broad shoulders?"

"Oh, God, yes," Micah whispered.

That ice had finally reached Greg's heart. "Then yeah, it's them." He felt sick to his stomach. "Fuck, just listen to them, laughing and joking. Why not? It's nearly Christmas, and a month or so ago, they beat up another fag. One less homo in the world, right?"

Micah's eyes widened. "They're getting up. They're going to leave."

Greg's heart pounded. "Follow them? See if they get into a vehicle? That way, we can get a license number."

Micah nodded. "I can do that. You stay here, okay? I'll be back. I don't know how long it will take, but you don't move from this spot, you hear me?"

Greg shivered. "Loud and clear." He didn't think he was capable of movement right then anyway.

Micah released Greg's hand, grabbed his jacket, and walked off. Greg didn't dare move, rooted to the bench. He reached for Micah's still half full glass, and drained it. The server approached him and refilled it.

How long he sat there, Greg had no idea. His lunch felt like a bowling ball in his stomach, and swallowing became a chore. When Micah's hand came to rest on his shoulder, he almost jumped out of his skin.

"Sorry." Micah slid into the booth next to him. "I've got it." He held up his phone. "Not only that, I took a photo of their car as they drove off." He squeezed Greg's shoulder. "You're absolutely positive it was them?"

Greg nodded. "No doubt at all."

"Then what do you want to do with this information?"

Greg had been thinking about that very thing. "We go home, and then I call Detective Riley. After that? I throw up." He felt like he was going to do that at any second.

"I'll pay the check, then I'll bring the car to the front of the restaurant. That's after I get you to the chairs by the door. Okay?" Micah gazed into his eyes.

Greg drew in a deep breath. "Okay." He just wanted to go home.

It wasn't until he was sitting by the door, waiting for Micah to appear, that he realized the truth of his statement. That house on Willow Creek Drive did feel like home. And that had everything to do with the people who lived in it.

One in particular.

Micah came into his dad's office, just in time to hear the tail end of Greg's conversation.

"Yes, thank you, Detective Riley. Yes, I'll be sure to give you a forwarding address when I leave here."

That was enough to make him stop listening, his heart sinking like a rock.

I'm deluding myself here, aren't I? This isn't some fairy tale. As soon as he's well enough to leave, Greg will pack his bag and that will be that. Gone.

It didn't matter that Micah was already head over heels in love for the first time in his life. This wasn't Greg's home, no matter how much it felt like he *belonged* there, heart, body and soul. He had his own family back in California, his own life to lead. And barring a miracle, or someone sprinkling fairy dust, there was nothing to keep Greg there.

There were no such things as miracles or magic.

"Micah?"

He pulled himself back into the moment. Dad was standing next to Greg, regarding Micah with amusement.

"Sorry, I must have zoned out there." Micah peered at Greg. "You look exhausted."

Greg gave him a weary smile. "Gee, thanks." Then he put his head back against the chair, closing his eyes.

Dad gazed at him in concern. "Micah's right, you're all wrung out. Why don't you go lie down for a while? We'll call you for dinner."

"Dad's right. A nap would do you good."

Greg opened his eyes and nodded. "Okay." Dad helped him to his feet, then handed him his crutches. Greg made his way around the desk, clearly fatigued. Micah followed him to his room, then guided him to sit on the bed.

"Lie back," he said, moving the crutches.

Greg didn't say a word, but merely shuffled up the bed until his head hit the pillows. Micah removed his boots, then went into the closet. He brought out a thick, soft comforter, and unfolded it, spreading it out over Greg's prone form. He bent low and stroked Greg's cheek. "Get some sleep."

"K." Greg already sounded half asleep. By the time Micah reached the door, his breathing had evened out. Micah pulled the door to, and walked into the kitchen. Dad was pouring out a mug of coffee. He glanced up as Micah entered.

"He looks awful."

"No wonder." Naomi shook her head. "How would you feel, if the assholes who beat you up and left you for dead were sitting a few feet behind you, eating away, happy as a clam? Poor Greg." Her face tightened. "What did the police say anyway?"

"They're gonna check the license and find out who the car is registered to. They already have Greg's descriptions. Then I guess we wait and see what they do next."

"Will Greg have to identify them in a line-up?"

"Probably. Thing is, what evidence is there likely to be after this time? It's just his word against theirs." Dad seemed miserable. Micah totally got that. He'd had the same thoughts all the trip home. Greg hadn't said a word, just stared through the windshield the whole time.

"Maybe it's enough to have them identified on record," he mused. "Because if they did this once, and got away with it, they might get the idea they can do it again. Their next victim might not be so lucky."

Naomi froze. "What are you talking about?"

It was then that Micah realized Naomi hadn't been home there when Greg had finally revealed what had happened. He sighed heavily. "Greg was targeted because he was gay."

Dad's face darkened. "I'm just glad he finally told the police everything. Not that it was a complete surprise. Didn't I guess back in that hospital room? Those hateful bastards." He glanced in the direction of Greg's room. "That boy didn't deserve this."

"*No one* deserves that!" Naomi yelled. Micah put his finger to his lips, and she stiffened. "Sorry. I got carried away. It's just that you think things are getting better, that we're advancing, but then you only have to click on a news site or open a newspaper to see we're actually moving backwards. It makes me sick to think there is so much *hate* out there." Her eyes glistened.

Micah strode across the kitchen and hugged her tightly. "It's six of one, half-dozen of the other, sis. You see the hate, but I see hope."

Naomi gaped at him. "Where?"

He cupped her chin. "When you talked about your classmates? I felt hopeful. You painted a picture of a diverse group, who all get along, in spite of what divides them, because they don't see the differences. That gives me hope, right there."

Naomi regarded him thoughtfully. "I didn't see it like that."

He kissed her cheek and released her. "But you do now." Micah smiled, then turned to his dad. "How would you feel if we put on a Christmas movie tonight? I was thinking popcorn too." This had to be Dad's decision.

Dad gazed at him for a moment. "We haven't watched one yet, have we?" When both of them shook their heads, he sighed. "Fair enough. Pick one." He snickered. "We're not exactly short on movies to choose from, right?" Mom's Christmas DVDs took up a whole shelf.

"Can I choose?" Naomi asked quietly.

Micah had a feeling he knew what was coming.

"Sure." Dad smiled. "It's not like we haven't seen all of them at least a gazillion times."

"It's A Wonderful Life," she announced promptly, her gaze flickering the tiniest bit in Micah's direction.

"Why not?" Dad agreed. Naomi beamed at him triumphantly.

Micah gave an inward groan. His sister was about as subtle as a sledgehammer.

Chapter Nineteen

Greg couldn't get rid of the idea that something was wrong with Micah. No, not just Micah—Joshua and Naomi too. There was nothing he could put his finger on, just an… undercurrent, a feeling throughout the day that something was going on beneath the surface, out of sight. Then it came to him, and he cursed himself for being so stupid.

Of course. Tomorrow is the anniversary of her death. No wonder they were distracted. He guessed it would be a while before Christmas regained any of its former magic and sparkle for the Trant family. They were working on it—well, Naomi certainly was—but Greg knew it wasn't going to be plain sailing. *Then I need to make the day as easy for them as I can.*

He just wasn't certain how he could accomplish that.

This is sure going to be one messed up Christmas.

He'd gotten over his shock of the previous day, but it hadn't entirely left his thoughts. Now and again he fell to wondering what was happening. Had the detectives taken the guys in for questioning, or would they leave it until after the holidays? Was there enough evidence to charge them? When would they need him to identify the bastards? The conversation with Detective Riley had brought one issue to the forefront of his mind, however—Micah.

Six weeks. That's all it's been, six weeks. Yet it felt like he'd known Micah for so much longer. A line came to mind from one of his mom's favorite musicals, My Fair Lady. Something about growing accustomed to someone's face, but there was more to it than that. Waking up in the morning and seeing Micah's smile. Hearing him laugh and joke with his dad. Watching him paint. Feeling that gentle hand on Greg's face when Micah kissed him.

Heat raced through him at the memory of other more carnal activities, but he knew his feelings weren't all about the sex. Yes, he'd experienced a lot of firsts with Micah, but that wasn't it either. When Detective Riley brought up the subject of Greg leaving Wyoming, that set off a chain reaction of conflicting emotions, which all boiled down to one vital realization.

Greg had no clue what to do.

He'd told himself it was no use making decisions right then. Those could wait. But he knew he was putting off the moment when he needed to decide where his future lay—and with whom. And as the day dragged on, those thoughts continued to plague him, until he couldn't take it any longer.

Inaction and indecision were no longer an option.

Greg tapped on Joshua's office door.

"Come in." Joshua was seated at his desk, peering at a monitor. Greg wasn't surprised to find him working: he guessed it was Joshua's way of coping. He smiled as Greg entered the room. "Hey. You need something?"

Greg hobbled over to the couch and sat down. "I was going to wrap my gifts, until I remembered I didn't buy any paper." He couldn't ask Micah: he'd locked himself away in his studio. Naomi had gone into Gillette for some last-minute groceries. It seemed like all the Trants were hiding from the holidays.

"No problem. We have tons of that. I'll find you a roll and some tape. Oh!" Joshua unlocked a drawer in his desk. "You might need this then." He removed a small silver bag. "The results of my little shopping trip for you."

"Great. Can we settle up? I can transfer the money to your account."

Joshua got up and walked over to him. "Yeah, sure." He handed Greg the bag, his expression thoughtful. "It's a sweet gift. Not what I expected you to get. Kinda made me feel like…" He sighed. "I wish I knew where this is going."

Greg didn't have to ask what 'this' referred to. "You and me both, sir." Joshua blinked, and Greg smiled. "No, I don't have the answers either." Then he remembered his real reason for paying Joshua a visit. "Can I ask a favor? Do you have a laptop I can use?" Thus far, he'd used Joshua's PC, but he didn't want to impost any further.

"Sure. I'll bring it to your room, along with the password details." He laid a hand on Greg's shoulder. "I know the circumstances that brought you here were pretty awful, but… I sure am glad you're here. It's been great having you around the place these last weeks." He swallowed. "And I'm gonna miss you when you leave. I know I won't be the only one."

Greg's throat tightened. "Please… don't."

Joshua flinched. "I'm sorry. Ignore me. I'm just a little frazzled right now. Time of year, an' all that." He took a deep breath. "Anyhow, if you go to your room, I'll bring you the paper, scissors, tape, and the laptop. That okay?"

Greg used the crutches to lever himself up onto his feet. "Thank you." Impulsively, Greg put his arm around Joshua's back and gave him a one-arm hug, as much as he dared do while trying not to overbalance. Then he took a careful step back.

Joshua's face flushed. "You're welcome."

Greg made his way to his bedroom, taking his time.

At least he was going to do *something*.

A CHRISTMAS PROMISE

When he'd lain awake for more than an hour, Micah decided enough was enough. He got out of bed, pulled on his robe, and crept downstairs. The house was silent, and through the windows he could see the bright lights that still burned. Then he realized: it was officially Christmas Day.

A wave of sorrow washed over him, and he fought back the tears. "Merry Christmas, Mom," he whispered. Fighting to maintain his composure, he went into the kitchen to make himself a warm drink. When a noise disturbed the silence, Micah knew he wasn't the only insomniac in the house. He crept to the hallway that led to the back yard. Light spilled from under Greg's bedroom door. Micah walked up to it, internally debating whether to knock, or just make his drink and go back to bed.

Like he could walk away, especially when he didn't want to be on his own right then.

Micah rapped gently on the door.

"Come in." He just about caught Greg's quietly spoken instruction. Micah pushed open the door and stepped inside.

The room was lit by the lamp next to Greg's bed. He lay under the comforter, no trace of sleep in his expression. "Hey. You couldn't sleep either?"

Micah smiled. "It's getting to be a habit."

"I didn't see much of you today." Greg patted the space beside him. "Please, sit."

Micah sat on the bed, leaning against the head board. "Sorry. I had something to do in the studio." He knew that was only half the truth, but Greg didn't need to know the rest, especially as most of it related to him.

"Did you get it done, whatever it was?"

He sighed. "Yes." He had no idea how it would be received, however. "And why can't you sleep?"

"Too much on my mind, I guess. I couldn't switch my brain off."

Micah came to a reluctant decision. "I should let you at least try to sleep." He got up.

"Do you have to go?" Greg blurted out. He paused, and Greg held out his hand. "Stay with me? Please?"

Slowly, Micah grasped it. "You sure?"

Greg nodded. In silence, he released Micah's hand and lifted the comforter and sheets, revealing his body, bare but for a pair of white boxers, and the ever-present cast.

Micah let his robe slip from his shoulders, then climbed into the bed, thankful that he was on Greg's right. "I don't want to accidentally nudge your leg or something."

Greg smiled. "You won't. You're careful." Micah liked the confidence that rang out in those few words.

Micah stretched out beside him, and Greg covered them both. He lay on his back, his head turned in Micah's direction.

"Do you know how many times this past week

that I've wanted to ask you to do this?" Greg chuckled softly. "Seems weird, huh? I know how your dick tastes, but I don't know how it feels to spend a night with you sleeping beside me."

Micah snickered. "Yeah, we *have* been doing that a lot, haven't we?" He reached across and brushed his fingers over Greg's nipples. "What about now? Is that all you wanna do? Sleep?"

Greg's breathing hitched and he shivered. "Why—what else did you have in mind?"

"That depends on you." Micah knew where he wanted this to go, but only if Greg was on the same page. Not to mention getting their heads around the logistics of the situation.

"So… if I wanted more than a midnight blow-job, you'd be okay with that?" Greg's eyes shone in the lamplight.

Fuck. Micah wasn't the only one who needed. Before he could reply, Greg grasped Micah's hand and pulled it down his torso, until his fingers touched the soft cotton of his boxers—and the hardness that lay beneath them.

The breath caught in Micah's throat. "And if I want this inside me?" Just the thought made him hot all over.

Greg's eyes were huge. "Can… can we do that? I mean, with my leg and all?"

Micah grinned. "Where there's a will…." Then sanity returned. "Only, I'll have to go back to my room for supplies."

"No need." Greg pointed to the nightstand. "There are condoms and lube in that drawer." When

Micah gazed at him inquiringly, he flushed. "So I was hopeful. Not to mention practical. Bite me."

Micah couldn't resist. "I was thinking more along the lines of sucking you, but whatever." Greg let out a dirty giggle. Then a thought occurred to him. "When did you buy those?"

"When you went to the restroom at CVS. And about that... damn, do you *always* pee so fast? I almost broke my other leg, trying to get back to where you left me, before you worked out where I was."

"I'll take my time in the future." Micah knelt up in bed and pulled back the sheets. "Okay, these need to come off." He grabbed the waistline on Greg's boxers and slowly eased them down, taking extra care when he got to the cast. Greg's dick stood upright, and Micah licked his lips. "Damn. Someone's in need."

"Micah?" He glanced down to where Greg stared up at him. "Kiss me?"

Like Micah could refuse that invitation.

He got off the bed and removed his own shorts, his cock already at half-mast. Greg held his arms wide, and Micah rejoined him, their bodies touching as he leaned over and took Greg's mouth in a languid kiss. Greg moaned softly, his hands caressing Micah's nape and shoulders, shuddering when Micah stroked lower.

"Love it... when you touch me," Greg said, a shiver coursing through him. "Love the way you kiss me too."

It was there, right there, on the tip of Micah's tongue. *That's because I love you.* Only he didn't dare. Instead, he kissed down the length of Greg's neck, feeling the tremors that rocketed through him. It was like each caress, each kiss, caused a physical reaction. Micah felt every explosion of sensation in Greg's body, and it sent his own desire spiraling. Then Greg grabbed him and tugged him higher, their mouths meeting in a heated fusion of lips and tongues. Micah explored him, his hand moving slowly over Greg's chest and abs, shifting lower, until that hard shaft was in his hand once more.

Only that wasn't where he wanted it. And Micah didn't want to wait any longer. He straddled Greg and leaned forward to kiss him. "You ready?"

Greg's chest rose and fell rapidly. "You're kidding, right? I think I'll blow the second I'm inside you."

Micah smiled. "We can always do it again, okay?"

A sigh shuddered out of him. "Yeah. Okay."

Micah reached for the lube and slicked up a couple of fingers. He lowered his head until his lips brushed against Greg's. "Kiss me," he whispered.

Greg let out a low moan, his hands on Micah's nape and head, pulling him into a deep, toe-curling kiss. Micah explored him leisurely, while reaching back to slide his fingers into his own ass.

"What are you doing back there?"

Micah grinned. "Something *you* get to do, another time." He ran his tongue over Greg's nipple, loving the shivers that multiplied through him. Then it was back to kissing, until both of them were breathless.

When they parted, Micah looked him in the eyes. "You are going to lie here and let me do all the work, you got that?" Greg made a soft noise at the back of his throat, and Micah stared at him. "I mean it. Keep that leg still." When Greg pulled a face, Micah whispered in his ear, "There will be other times, baby. I promise. But for now, I don't want you hurting. Okay?"

Greg's gaze locked on his. "Okay." His lips twitched. "*Now* can we make love?"

Micah's heart soared at Greg's words. "God, yes."

Greg wanted to slow down time, to savor the moment, but all too soon, he was lost in the heat and tightness of Micah's body as he slowly impaled himself on Greg's gloved dick. Greg held still, badly wanting to move, but not daring. He loved how Micah bided his time, carefully lowering himself until at last, Greg was inside him. The sensations took his breath away.

Then Micah began to move, a slow rocking back and forth, his hands on Greg's chest, and *fuck*, that was exquisite. Greg grabbed Micah's ass, caressing and squeezing the firm flesh, crying out when Micah's movements sped up. "Oh, God."

Above him, Micah nodded. "I know. Feels so good." He wrapped one hand around his own dick, tugging.

"Too good," Greg groaned. "Not sure if I can—" And then Greg was coming, balls tingling as he filled the condom, stifling the urge to thrust up into Micah, his body jolted over and over again. Micah was shaking, his hand a blur on his cock.

"In my mouth," Greg cried out. "Micah!"

Micah didn't hesitate. He held his dick steady, shooting his load in an arc that landed on Greg's chest, chin and lips. He scooped up come and fed it to Greg, who sucked on his fingers, cleaning them with his tongue.

Micah lay down beside him, and removed the condom. After dropping it into the small trashcan beside the bed, he pressed up against Greg's body, both of them warm and damp.

"That was over *way* too fast," Greg murmured sleepily.

Micah craned his neck and kissed Greg on the lips. "Then the next time will be better. And the time after that. And the time after that…."

Greg gave a drowsy chuckle. "Like the way you think."

Micah pulled the comforter over them, and rested his head on Greg's shoulder. Greg breathed in Micah's scent, and let out a soft sigh of contentment, before drifting off into a deep, velvety sleep.

K.C. WELLS

Chapter Twenty

Micah woke up to find a warm body snuggled against him, and it was heaven. About as heavenly as the memories of the two of them, making love. He could still recall the expression of awe and sheer pleasure on Greg's face as he came. His disgruntled comments about the speed of it all had been comical.

Micah wouldn't have changed one second of it. Those intimate moments had been like nothing he'd ever experienced, and he could only think of one thing to account for that.

This is what it must feel like to make love, not just have sex. To have the heart engaged, as well as the body.

Then it hit him. He'd spent the night in Greg's room, and that was bound to be noticed. Dad was a creature of habit, after all.

Micah listened intently. From the kitchen came faint voices, and the unmistakable aroma of roasting turkey that seeped under the closed door.

It was official. They were in trouble.

He nudged Greg gently. "Hey, sleepyhead."

Greg shifted, soft noises escaping as he reached for Micah. "Hey. Morning."

"Never mind morning. It's gone nine o'clock already."

Greg's eyes popped open. "What?"

Micah nodded. "They've already got the turkey in the oven." Naomi was never going to let him forget this. And as for Dad? It was bad enough he'd caught them in the bathroom together.

Greg sat up slowly. "I slept like a log. It was wonderful." Then he clammed up when someone knocked on the door.

"Boys?" Dad coughed. "There are two mugs of coffee out here on the hall table. Whenever you're ready."

"What do you mean, whenever they're ready?" Naomi called out from the kitchen. "We're sitting around here, waiting for those two so we can—" Seconds later there was a loud rap on the door. "Get your butts out here. I am *not* doing this all by myself, because do you really want Dad cooking? And there are presents to be opened, for God's sake!" Loud snorts and mutterings grew quieter as she stomped off down the hall.

Dad cleared his throat. "What she said." Then there was silence.

Micah glanced at Greg, who promptly burst out laughing. "Well, that's *us* told." He bit his lip and wrinkled his nose. "I don't know about you, but I really need a shower."

Micah nodded. "You go shower. I'll go upstairs—after I've calmed the storm out there." Before he could climb out of bed, Greg laid a gentle hand on his arm.

"In case I forget to tell you? Last night was… awesome. Every single minute of it. And that includes falling asleep with you."

Naomi be damned. Micah pushed Greg's tousled hair away from his face, leaned in, and kissed him, a chaste, sweet kiss that was more 'you-are-adorable' than 'let's-do-it-all-again.' "You felt amazing. And I loved curling up with you."

Greg's face flushed. "And if you need anything today, just ask, all right?"

Micah kissed his cheek, then got out of bed. He pulled on his robe, and cautiously opened the door. There was no one in sight. Micah turned and smiled at Greg. "The coast is clear."

Greg chuckled. "Don't forget your coffee."

Micah closed the door and stepped into the hallway. It wasn't until he was at the kitchen door, a mug in his hand, that the significance of Greg's words struck him.

Mom. And I'd forgotten. Then he realized something. The pain and grief that had numbed him the previous Christmas was still present, but robbed of its

intensity somehow. *It's true. Time is a great healer.*
Only, Micah knew it was more than that. He would
always have his memories, but now he wanted to make
new ones—with Greg.

And how long will it be before he leaves?

Just like that, Micah's newfound peace deserted
him.

He entered the kitchen, his heart heavy. Dad was
cracking eggs into a bowl. He glanced up as Micah
approached. "Well, good morning." Another glance, this
time to the wall clock. "Yep, it's still morning."

"Merry Christmas to you too, Dad."

"Yeah, yeah." Dad snickered and went back to
his eggs. Across the table from him, still dressed in her
red pajamas, Naomi glared.

"And where's the other one?"

"Having a shower." Micah knew exactly what
was going on. Naomi was simply swapping her grief for
another strong emotion, and feigned anger would do just
as well. He met her gaze and nodded once, just to let her
know he was on to her. "Merry Christmas, sis."

Naomi got up from her chair, walked over to him,
and hugged him tightly. "Right back atcha," she
whispered. Naomi released him and stepped back,
coughing. "Dad decided to make breakfast this morning.
Be afraid. Be very afraid."

Dad brandished his fork. "Remarks like that will
result in certain people being put on vegetable
preparation duty, and that may even include doing the
dishes."

Naomi smiled sweetly. "That's what we have a
dishwasher for."

Dad's smile was equally sweet. "And your father is very handy with a wrench. Bear that in mind. Appliances have been known to break down when you least expect it." He chuckled when Naomi gasped, and winked at Micah. "That shut her up." He laid his fork on the countertop. "I'll wait until Greg's out of the shower before I start cooking. Call me when you're ready to eat." And with that, he left the kitchen.

Naomi gave Micah an innocent look. "Thought you'd give water conservation a miss this time, huh?" She pushed her tongue into her cheek.

Micah fired her a warning glance, before staring in the direction of Dad's office. "How is he this morning?" he asked quietly.

Naomi's mood changed instantly. She sighed. "I tried to keep him focused on other things—and thank you for that, by the way. He came downstairs to tell me you weren't in your room. Didn't take him long to figure out where you were."

"Was he okay about it?" Micah could only imagine what had gone through his dad's head.

"Surprisingly, yeah." Naomi smiled. "Something else I have to thank you for."

"Huh?"

"You've kinda paved the way for when I invite Si—when I invite someone to stay here."

"Oh really?" Micah grinned. "All right, who is he?"

Naomi sniffed. "I plead the Fifth."

Micah snorted. "You're pre-med, not pre-law. And you know I'll get it out of you, one way or another."

"You can try," she said in a sing-song voice.

"Now get your butt upstairs and get cleaned up, so we can open some goddamn presents." She gave him another glare. "At this rate it'll be midnight before you get your act together."

He laughed and headed for the stairs. When he reached his room, he closed the door behind him and leaned against it.

He had the feeling it was going to be a long, long day.

Naomi collected the plates and mugs, and loaded them into the dishwasher. "Okay," she said triumphantly. "*Now* can we open presents?"

Joshua shook his head. "I knew I shouldn't have put them under the tree before I went to bed," he told Greg and Micah. "She's been like a six-year-old since she got up and saw them."

Greg sighed. "I did the same thing last night."

"In that case, let's just give her the wrapping paper from ours, and she can play with that." Micah gave Naomi an innocent smile. "You'd be happy with that, right, sis?"

Greg snorted when he saw the glare Naomi gave her brother. "Yeah, right. I wouldn't say stuff like that if she was my sister. I like my balls where they are." Then he realized what he'd said, and he widened his eyes. "Oh, God. I'm sorry. That just slipped out."

Joshua stared at him for a moment, and then guffawed. "No need to apologize, son. You're sorta one of the family now."

Greg didn't miss the way Micah's face tightened. *What was that?* But before he could analyze it further, Naomi dove out of the room, heading for the living room.

Joshua sighed. "No point putting off the inevitable, I guess." He followed her out of the room.

Now that was a reaction Greg understood. This had to be hard on Joshua: a time of joy mingled with sorrow. For a moment he found himself thinking about his own dad. *I wish we could have shared one more Christmas.* Not that he could recall the Christmases from his childhood. Apart from their initial meeting, their brief time together had only spanned the five months leading up to his death.

Micah's hand was at his elbow. "Come on, Hopalong. Let's go sit in front of the fire and see what Santa has brought."

"I know what *I* want for Christmas," Greg murmured. When Micah gazed at him quizzically, he smiled. "More nights like last night."

"I think that can be arranged," Micah said softly. His face tightened for a fleeting moment, then straightened. "Although I doubt you'll find that under the tree."

Greg doubted it too.

He followed Micah into the living room, where the tree was already a blaze of light and color, and the fire pushed out warmth into every corner. Joshua was in his armchair, and Greg's footrest stood next to the couch. He sat down, lifting his leg up onto the pillows, Micah beside him.

Naomi knelt on the floor at the foot of the tree, peering at the prettily wrapped packages.

"Seeing as I'm still in my red jammies, I'll play Santa." She picked up one present, and Greg recognized it. "For Joshua, from Greg." Naomi weighed it experimentally in one hand. "Ooh, heavy." She passed it to Joshua, before picking up a smaller package. "Another from Greg, this time for Micah." Her eyes gleamed. "Wonder what's inside?" She shook it.

"Hand it over, *Santa.*" Micah held out his hand.

She huffed, but did as instructed. "And here's one for Greg, from Micah. Another heavy one." She got up and brought it over to him, before diving back to the tree. "Aha! One for me—a light, squishy one, from Greg."

For the next minute or so, the only sound in the room was that of tearing paper. Joshua cackled. "A cookbook?" He peered at Greg, grinning. "You trying to tell me something, son?"

Greg shrugged. "I figured you might have had enough of these two insulting you all the time. Maybe it's time to show them what you're made of."

Joshua nodded, his eyes gleaming. "Exactly. And I get to experiment on them too." He regarded Greg warmly. "Thank you."

"Oh, these are great!" She held up the T-shirts for her dad to see. One had *MEH* in large letters across the front, another had *In Memory Of When I Cared*, and the third, *This Is What AWESOME looks like*. She beamed at Greg. "These are so me!"

He had to laugh at her reaction. "Funny—that thought occurred to me too."

Naomi flew across the space between them and hugged him. "Thank you. Wow, you got to know me so fast!" When she released him, she leaned forward and kissed his cheek. "So glad you're here. It's gonna be such a pity when you have to leave."

For a second, Greg's heart stuttered, but he said nothing. Everything was still up in the air.

"Oh, Greg. It's beautiful," Micah said in an awed tone. He held the stainless-steel bracelet, inset with pieces of abalone.

"I wanted to get you something that an artist would appreciate. The colors in the abalone are just gorgeous."

Micah nodded. "I agree. But... when did you get this?"

Joshua coughed. "He may have had a little help."

Micah laughed, and leaned across to kiss Greg, not on the cheek as Naomi had done, but on the mouth. Nor was it a peck on the lips either.

Micah kissed him like a lover.

It took Greg all of one second to respond, lifting his hands to cup Micah's face. He wasn't going to hide his feelings, not after that display of affection. When Micah broke the kiss, he stared at Greg. "Wow."

Greg smiled. "Ditto." He tore the wrapping paper from the heavy square package, to find a plain white box, filled with polystyrene pieces. Carefully he removed the top layer, to see the gleam of glass. He removed the rest of the packaging, and lifted out the object. "It's a snow globe." Then he frowned. "Isn't that the Devil's Tower?" Around the thick base was emblazoned the word, Wyoming.

"Yup." Micah gave a nod of approval. "I'm impressed that you recognize it."

Greg had to chuckle. "One of my favorite movies of all time is Close Encounters of the Third Kind." He turned the globe upside down. "Aw, damn."

"What's wrong?"

He grinned. "I was looking for the key to turn, so it could play de-de-de-de-deeeee. And the only way you could improve on this? Instead of snow floating around it, it should have little glittery UFOs."

Micah smiled. "I wanted to give you something to remember your stay in Wyoming. So... do you like it?"

Greg kissed him on the lips. "I love it. Not that I needed something to remind me of Wyoming." Micah had already claimed his heart.

Naomi's impatient, loud sigh broke the moment. "When you two have finished, Misters Kissy McKissy Face..."

Greg laughed so hard, he almost coughed up a lung.

Micah got up from the couch. "I haven't wrapped your present yet, Dad. I just need to go find it." He left the living room.

Joshua put down his cookery book. "Thank you," he said quietly, not meeting their gaze. "Today was never gonna be easy, but this is better than I thought it would be. For the first time in a long while, I feel like your mom wouldn't be pissed if she walked through that door. She might even smile." He gazed at the tree. "And she'd love this."

Naomi got up and moved to sit beside his

armchair, her head on his knee. Joshua stroked her long hair. Silence fell, but it wasn't awkward.

Micah walked into the room, holding a large, flat object, and Greg knew immediately what it was. He handed it to his dad. "I only finished it last night, so it's not ready for hanging yet, but…"

Joshua stared at the portrait, his brown eyes large and round. Tears rolled down his cheeks, and he wiped them away. "Oh, Micah. It's her. It's really her." He lifted his head and smiled. "Thank you, son. You couldn't have chosen a more perfect gift." Carefully he put down the canvas and stood up, his arms wide. Micah stepped into the circle of those arms and they hugged in silence.

Greg watched them, his heart aching. The love they shared, and the ways in which they shared it, was nothing short of wonderful. If anything, the sight only firmed his resolve.

I'm doing the right thing. I hope.

The center of the table was so full, it was difficult to find a spot that wasn't covered by a dish or plate of food. A gloriously brown turkey, its skin crisp and succulent, sat in front of Dad. A deep bowl of mashed potatoes, another with carrots, and yet another with turnips and parsnips, surrounded it. Cranberry sauce, gravy and dressing filled up the gaps. Naomi had brought out the wedding china, white with a gold trim, and the best wine glasses. The silverware gleamed. Tall red candles stood in elegant candlesticks, their flames flickering, the light dancing on the walls. Micah sat facing his dad, Naomi to his right and Greg to his left.

It was perfect. Well, almost.

Micah raised his glass. "To family." His words echoed around the table. The toast over, he sipped the chilled white wine, relishing its citrus flavors. Then he smiled. "I'm starved," he lied.

Naomi snorted. "No change there then." Then she attacked her turkey with gusto.

Greg hadn't taken a bite yet.

Micah indicated the food with his fork. "Hey, come on. We slaved all afternoon on this."

Greg put down his wine glass and stared at him. "What's wrong?"

Micah blinked. "Wrong? Nothing's wrong." His pulse sped up.

"Sure." Greg folded his arms. "That's why I've had this feeling all day that you're hiding something. Several times I caught you looking at me, and you seemed so... sad. And before you remind me what today is, no, it's not that. It's something to do with me."

"Don't do this. Not now." Micah set his jaw. It was *Christmas Day*, for God's sake, a day that held enough pain for them. He wasn't about to add to that by spoiling the atmosphere with an outburst.

Greg stared at him. "Do you really think I could enjoy this food, knowing you're hiding something from me? Like I can't see it in your face? Tell me, Micah. Please?"

Micah drew in a deep breath. "Do you really

want to know?" He pushed his plate aside. "Of *course* I'm sad. Because right now, this is perfect. Dad got it right this morning. You're one of the family now."

Greg arched his eyebrows. "And this makes you sad?"

"You're damn straight I'm sad!" Micah fought to draw breath into his lungs. "Because there will come a day when you leave here. I've known that ever since you spoke with that detective. And when you walk out that door, you'll be taking my goddamn heart with you!" His chest heaved, and his throat hurt, but they were as nothing compared to the ache in his heart.

Dad's breathing caught, and beside him, Naomi smothered a gasp, her fork clanging as it hit her plate.

Greg gaped at him. "That's it? That's what's bothering you?" He shook his head. "Why in hell would I want to leave here, when that means leaving you?"

Micah froze. "What?"

"Don't you think those same thoughts haven't been going through *my* head too? But there was damn all I could do about it, not while I'm still banged up like this. That didn't stop me from doing a little research." Greg glanced across the table to Naomi. "Could you go to my room, please, and fetch your dad's laptop from the nightstand?"

"Sure." Naomi scooted away from the table.

Dad cleared his throat. "I didn't want to say anything before now, but—"

"You didn't have to," Greg interjected. "I got the message loud and clear yesterday. You didn't say it in so many words, but the meaning was clear—'You're gonna hurt my son.' And I couldn't do that, sir. How could I hurt him?" Greg's gaze met Micah's. "I love him."

Everything just… stopped.

"You love me?"

Greg smiled. "Of course I love you. You're amazing. I've only scratched the surface of knowing you, and I can't wait to learn more." He stilled, and Micah knew what he was waiting for.

Slowly, he reached for Greg's hand. "I love you too. And I don't want to lose you."

Naomi gave a little sob from the doorway. "That was probably the most beautiful thing I've ever heard." She came over to Greg and handed him the laptop, before bending low to kiss his cheek. Then she scooted back to her chair.

Greg pushed his plate to one side to make room. He booted up the laptop, then turned it to show Micah a series of bookmarks. "Look at these vacancies. Product Manager. Efficiency Consultant. Account Manager. Pretty much any corporate job I can find. Do you know what doors an MBA opens? Oh, Lord, just about anything." He grinned. "And these are just the tip of the iceberg."

Micah peered at the screen. "These… these are all companies in Wyoming."

Greg's grin hadn't diminished. "Duh. Why would I look anywhere else, when I already have a house in this State? A house, I might add, with a large upstairs room that gets lots of natural light. Perfect for turning into, say, an artist's studio." He reached for Micah's hand. "That's if there's an artist who wants to come live with me. Know anyone who might be interested?"

Micah caught his breath. "Seriously?"

Greg nodded. "I don't know when—or even if—this police business will get cleared up, but I'm prepared for whatever happens. What I am *not* prepared for, however, is leaving this house without you at my side."

"I wouldn't hold my breath if I were you," Naomi said quietly. "Wyoming doesn't have a hate crimes statute."

Greg breathed deeply. "Then we'll prosecute them for assault if we can. But that doesn't matter right now. All that matters right now is Micah's answer." He locked gazes with him. "Want to start a new life with me?"

Micah laced their fingers and smiled. "That's the best Christmas present you could ever give me." He got up, moved closer, and leaned over to kiss Greg on the lips, not bothering how long it lasted.

Until Dad coughed. "Not that I wanna interrupt or anything, but our Christmas dinner is getting cold."

"And considering how much time I spent on it, I'm gonna be pissed if it's ruined just because you two can't keep your hands off each other," Naomi added.

Micah broke the kiss, chuckling. "Point taken." He sat down, unable to tear his gaze away from Greg. Micah smiled. "I seem to have gotten my appetite back."

"I'd like to propose a toast." Greg raised his wine glass. "To Joshua and Hayden, who brought us together."

Joshua swallowed. "I hope wherever he is, he's at peace. Because his letter brought a little of that into my life."

Micah echoed Greg's toast, his heart soaring with joy. Right then, he had so much to be thankful for.

Micah rolled over in bed, and encountered cool sheets where Greg had lain. He sat up in bed, rubbing his eyes. The blue LED display showed it to be two in the morning.

Greg was sitting in a chair, facing the window, wrapped in a comforter. Outside, the world was an almost eerie blue, moonlight reflecting off the snow.

"Hey. Couldn't you sleep?"

Greg turned his head toward Micah and smiled. "It's snowing."

Micah chuckled. "Yeah, well, it does that a lot around here." He shook his head. "Although I don't suppose you have much snow in California."

"Not really." Greg's eyes shone in the reflected light. "But I could get used to it." He sighed. "I'm sorry about the way I sprung things on you at dinner. I wasn't going to say anything until I had something definite to share, but there was no way I could keep quiet when you were clearly hurting."

Micah got out of bed and knelt beside Greg's chair. "I understand that now."

Greg stroked his hair. "And besides, there's a lot to do before we can even think about moving. It'll probably be summer before we finally move to Jackson."

Micah blinked. "Summer?"

Greg chuckled. "Yes, Mr. Artist. *Someone* has a show this spring in Gillette, remember?"

What amazed Micah was that he *had* forgotten. "Okay, you got a point there."

"And then there's my mom to consider. We need to take a trip to California, but that's after I break the good news to her. I don't want your first visit to be too much of a shock."

"Yeah, that might be a good idea." From everything Greg had said, it didn't sound like his mom was going to freak out.

Greg gestured to his leg. "*This* is what needs to happen first. Once the cast is off, and I'm fully mobile, then I can start filling out those job applications in earnest. And I'm not going to do that if I'm not one hundred percent fit." He gazed out at the snow. "You'll love Jackson. The Teton Pass is so beautiful. Just think of it. A whole new world to explore and be inspired by."

"Talking of exploring… come back to bed?" Micah grasped his hand.

Greg nodded, and Micah helped him back to the bed. He pulled the comforter high, then snuggled up to him, his head on Greg's chest. "I think until we move? I'm sharing your room. It's easier than trying to get you up the stairs."

Greg snickered. "You're not thinking about those stairs. You're thinking about putting more distance between us and your dad and sister."

Micah snorted. "Hey, you know what they're like. Do you blame me? At one point this evening, after dinner, it actually crossed my mind to move us into the studio."

Greg stilled. "Seriously?"

"Uh huh. I thought about it for all of ten seconds,

before I realized the only place I could put a bed would be up the ladder on the higher level, and somehow I couldn't see you climbing that every night."

"Only if you want me to break the other leg." Greg put his arm around Micah and held him close. "This will do just fine."

A comfortable silence fell, and Micah drank in Greg's reassuring presence, his warmth, the feel of his body against Micah's. A drowsiness stole over him, helped by the beat of Greg's heart against his ear. "You wanna know what I was thinking about that night, right before I found you?"

"What?" Greg sounded equally sleepy.

"My mom. I guess it makes me happy to think she had a hand in this somehow. Like she was bringing us together." He chuckled. "Maybe Naomi was right after all."

"About what?"

"Oh, she was talking about the magic of Christmas. I told her there was no such thing. Well, looks like I got it wrong. Christmas works its own magic." He chuckled again. "Only don't tell her I said that."

Greg kissed the top of his head, his hand moving gently on Micah's back. "Your secret is safe with me." He sighed. "I believe in magic and miracles."

"You do?"

"Sure. What was you finding me that night, if it wasn't a miracle? Of course, there *is* an alternative theory."

"Oh?"

Greg sighed, his breath stirring Micah's hair. "Maybe this is Fate stepping in."

"What do you mean?"

"Our dads never got the chance to see where their love might take them. Maybe we've been given that chance. I for one, want to make sure we never waste a moment of the time given to us." He tilted Micah's chin and kissed him on the lips. "And that's a promise," he whispered.

The End

By K.C. Wells

A CHRISTMAS PROMISE

(K.C. Wells & Parker Williams)
Endings and Beginnings
(K.C. Wells & Parker Williams)

Un Coeur Déverrouillé
Croire en Thomas

Secrets – with Parker Williams
Before You Break
An Unlocked Mind

Personal
Making it Personal
Personal Changes
More than Personal
Personal Secrets
Strictly Personal
Personal Challenges

Une Affaire Personnelle
Changements Personnels
Plus Personnel
Secrets Personnels
Strictement Personnel

Una Questione Personale
Cambiamenti Personali
Piú che personale
Segreti Personali
Strettamente personale

Es wird persönlich

K.C. WELLS

Persönliche Veränderungen
Mehr als Persönliche
Persönliche Geheimnisse
Streng Persönlich

Confetti, Cake & Confessions
Confetti, Coriandoli e Confessioni

Connections
Connexion

Saving Jason
Per Salvare Jason
Jasons Befreiung

Island Tales

Waiting for a Prince
September's Tide
Submitting to the Darkness

Le Maree di Settembre
In Attesa di un Principe

Lightning Tales
Teach Me
Trust Me
See me
Love Me

Lehre Mich
Vertau Mir

A CHRISTMAS PROMISE

Sieh Mich
Liebe Mich

Il Professore
Fidati di me

A Material World
Lace
Satin
Silk

Spitze

Double or Nothing
Back from the Edge
Switching it up
Scambio di ruoli

Anthologies

Fifty Gays of Shade
Winning Will's Heart

Who is Tantalus?

For those who like their stories intensely erotic, featuring hot men and even hotter sex....
Who don't mind breaking the odd taboo now and again....
Who want to read something that adds a little heat to their fantasies....
...there's Tantalus.
Because we all need a little tantalizing.
Tantalus is the hotter, more risqué alter ego of K.C. Wells
Amazon page:
https://www.amazon.com/Tantalus/e/B01IN33IZO

Playing with Fire (Damon & Pete)
A series of (so far) four short gay erotic stories:
Summer Heat
After
Consequences
Limits

About the Author

K.C. Wells started writing in 2012, although the idea of writing a novel had been in her head since she was a child. But after reading that first gay romance in 2009, she was hooked.

She now writes full time, and the line of men in her head, clamouring to tell their story, is getting longer and longer. If the frequent visits by plot bunnies are anything to go by, that's not about to change anytime soon.

E-mail: **k.c.wells@btinternet.com**

Facebook: **https://www.facebook.com/KCWellsWorld**

Twitter: @K_C_Wells

Website: **http://www.kcwellsworld.com**

Instagram: **https://www.instagram.com/k.c.wells/**

Blog: **http://kcwellsworld.blogspot.com**

Printed in Great Britain
by Amazon